Adonis & Venus 2

A D.C. Love Story

By: Ty Leese Javeh

Text **Treasured** to **22828**

To subscribe to our Mailing

List.

Interested in becoming a

part of the Treasured

Publications family?

Submit manuscripts to

Info@Treasuredpub.com

Acknowledgments

I thank God for all my blessings and for always guiding me. My publisher Treasure of Treasured publications for believing in me. I would like to thank Royalty Publishing House for giving me this opportunity. Of course my wonderful support team my sister's Samantha, Sabrina, Ladonna, and Shanika. My daughter and granddaughter Tilysha and Teliyah for being the reason I push to achieve success. My niece and nephew Ricky, Daria, for loving me no matter how crazy and silly I can be. My pen sisters Ms. T Nicole, Reign, Khamesia, Taucita, and Authoress Nicole Dior for allowing me to bother you daily with ideas or read this to see if it sounds good. I still stayed in you guys in box and emails. We pulled each other through the tough times and I thank you for being there and for encouraging and believing that I could do this. Ashley, Kevin, Andrea, Sekenah, and Keisha thanks for the many times I called, sent a text, or in box interrupting you at work with my thoughts and ideas for this book and for encouraging me every time I doubt myself. A for the readers: Thank you so much for reading my work, and following me and supporting me as a new author. A special thanks to Milly Montana for allowing me to use the lyrics to Just want the Money from his mixtape *Backfrmthefeds* available on spinrilla.

A note from the Author:

I am still learning my craft and appreciate all those who have given me advice or help me understand what I needed to do to build myself as and author. Check out my other books available on Amazon, and Barnes & Noble

Survivor of Love 1 and 2

Adonis & Venus 1 and 2

Contact Ty Leese Javeh:

Facebook: tyleesejaveh

Twitter: @tyleesejaveh

Instagram: @tyleesejaveh

Wwwtyleesejaveh.webs.com

Synopsis

After the tragic death of his brother Lavelle, Adonis wants revenge. He blames Frank and his son

Maurice for Lavelle's death, and would not stop at nothing to take them down. When an old friend visits and find out the details of Lavelle's murder, Adonis has to search through all the lies to find the truth.

With a blossoming career, growing family, and a newfound independence, Venus is finally ready for a future with Adonis, but finding out that he has another woman pregnant kills all her hopes and dreams for the two of them. She's been hurt too many times by Adonis and decides to end the relationship for good, but the love she has for him is too strong and makes it difficult for her to walk away.

Loco and Kay Kay's relationship has them both in a different place in life, doing things for each other that they wouldn't normally do. They bring out the best and worst in each other, but a possible pregnancy causes them to reflect on promises they made to themselves that have the two of the bumping heads.

Will the couples find a way to work past the problems and stay together, or are their problems too much for them to handle? Will Adonis make a mistake by putting his differences aside to join forces with an unexpected person and take over an empire, or will it be the best decision he can make? With so many secrets and lies being revealed, Adonis' anger surfaces and causes him to act out in ways that put him in danger; will he be able to come out of the dangerous situations that surround him, or will Venus pay the ultimate price for his anger? Sex, lies, secrets, jealousy, and new additions to the family all await you in the pages of this book.

Prologue

Adonis

I couldn't shake the eerie feeling that swept over me as I sat in the car waiting for Lavelle. Something wasn't right; I could feel it in my bones. My stomach churned like butter as my breathing made it hard for me to swallow. I took several deep breaths, tryna calm my nerves. The feeling was sickening. Something was telling me that I needed to find my brother. I stared out of the window tryna decide if I should stay in the car or go find my brother. It was dark as hell out here, and I couldn't see shit. I didn't fuck around in areas I wasn't familiar with; you never knew who the fuck was lurkin' around. I unlocked the door and took the keys out of the ignition.

"Fuck this waitin' shit."

I was going to find my fuckin' brother. I wasn't about to leave my brother out here with the wolves. I was my brother's keeper, and he was mine.

POW! POW! POW!

Gunshots rang out, cutting through the silence. My heart dropped, feeling like it stopped beating. I hopped out of the car and took off running in the direction that Lavelle had gone.

Everything seemed to be moving in slow motion as I ran toward the condemned building. Silence surrounded me with every step as adrenaline shot through my heart. I sped up my pace. I could hear my footsteps beating the pavement like a drum. I wiped the beads of sweat from my brows. I could feel a knot form in the back of my throat as I approached the entrance. I snatched the door open and couldn't believe my eyes. Lavelle was lying on the ground in a pool of his own blood, chest heaving, coughing, and struggling to breathe.

"LAAAAVEEEELLLLLLEEEEE!"

My voice sounded warped in my ears as I screamed his name. My heart was thumping through my ears as I rushed over to him. I fell to my knees. Chills ran through my body as I placed his head on my lap. His chest was rising and falling hard as he struggled for air. He was making a gurgling sound like he was drowning.

"HEEEEELLLLLPPPP!" I screamed, but there was no one around to hear my call. A tear escaped my eye as I began to speak.

"Please Lavelle, don't do this to me. you can't leave me."

The rest of my tears came rushing out like a storm of pain. I grabbed Lavelle's hand and squeezed it. My ribcage throbbed as I struggled to breathe. Thoughts of life with my brother invaded my mind as the tears continue to pour. I wipe the dripping snot from my nose, tasting the saltiness of my tears as I continued speaking.

"Please don't die on me, Lavelle. I don't know what I would do without you. You're all I got. I need you," I pleaded as my heart was slowly breaking.

I used my shirt to try to wipe away the bubbling blood that was shooting out of his mouth like a fountain. He tried to squeeze my hand, but it was barely noticeable. I laid my forehead on top of his and for the first time in my life, I prayed.

"God, if you can hear me like my momma say, then please don't take my brother away from me. I need him. I promise that if you do this for me, I will always honor you. I will do everything in my power to prove to you that I am worthy of your grace and mercy. Please let him survive. I can't live without him," I begged as tears formed a pool on top of his head.

My prayer was too late. Lavelle coughed up one last glob of blood, then his body went limp and lifeless. I tried to call out to him, but I could not form words. The pain in my heart spilled over to my chest. I clenched my chest as I balled up beside him in the fetal position. The pain I felt gripped my heart 'til all I could do was lay beside him, not wanting to leave him like a piece of trash that niggas stepped over in the street

"I love you." I whispered as I laid my head on his chest hoping that he heard me.

I tightened my grip around him and let out a scream. I felt like I was that ten-year-old little boy missing his father all over again only this was worse. My life was just swept from under me like a rug. I wanted to die with him. I knew that the emptiness that I was feeling in my heart would never be filled. Feeling rage growing in my heart with every beat, I struggled to catch my breath. I looked at my brother's lifeless body that rage turned back into pain. I pulled myself up on all fours trying to get up but I felt too weak to stand. I burst into tears. Slob started shooting out of my mouth like I was vomiting violently as I sat back down. pulled my knees to my chest and rocked myself staring emotionless at my brother's dead body.

"WHAT THE FUCK!" I heard a familiar voice shout from the entrance of the building.

I looked up and Maurice was standing with his hands on his head, tears forming in his eyes. I tried to respond, but I couldn't form the words. He rushed over to me, patting me down like he was the police. I pushed him away from me. That's when I noticed that I was covered in Lavelle's blood. I started hyperventilating, and the tears flooded my face once again.

"Come on, Adonis; we need to go." Maurice's voice was in a panic as he tried pulling me off the ground.

"NO, I am not leaving my brother!" I snapped, snatching away from him.

"Adonis, the police is coming, we got to go," he warned as sirens sounded from a distance. I didn't care if the police were coming or not; I wasn't leaving my brother lying in a dirty condemned building like one of the dead rats in the corner

"I SAID I'M NOT LEAVIN' MY FUCKIN' BROTHER!" I yelled. Maurice stood frozen for a few seconds, then he grabbed my brother's gun from his side and got the hell outta the building. I was numb and unaware of my surroundings. I didn't hear the police cars pull up, or the officers storm in the building.

"DON'T FUCKIN' MOVE!" shouted a police officer. I looked up and saw that four officers were standing a few feet away with their guns pointed at me.

"This is my brother, I didn't do nothing," I said, raising my hands above my head. Two of the officers grabbed me, slammed me to the ground, handcuffed, then searched me. I stared at my brother the whole time they were manhandling me.

Sitting handcuffed in the back of the police car, I watched as the cops and the medical examiner moved around collecting evidence and examining my brother's body; it was like watching a movie. The shit was unreal to me. Officer Wittman came to the car.

"I got this, Adonis; just play along," he whispered as he took the cuffs off of me. He pretended to be getting a statement from me, then handed me his card.

"You're free to go, but here's my card if you think of anything else." I nodded my head, my never leaving Lavelle's lifeless body. I walked over as they zipped the bag, my heart in pieces. I leaned on officer Wittman not being able control my emotions, tears fell from my eyes.

"I'm sorry this happened, your brother was a great man. I promise, we will find who did this," he assured as he patted me on the shoulder. I wiped my bloody hands on my shirt, then ran my hands down my face. I could smell his cologne mixed with blood on my hands. I closed my eyes, took a deep breath, then walked away.

Walking to Lavelle's truck was the longest walk of my life. I could barely lift my legs as I opened the door to get in the truck. I looked around at the building and the cops one last time before climbing in the driver's side. I chuckled to myself thinking he would never let me drive his baby.

"This shit is crazy," I blurted as I laid my head on the headrest and closed my eyes. I needed a minute to get myself together so I could drive.

Each adjustment to the seat and mirrors hurt like hell. I put the key in the ignition and started the car. Jay Z's "This Can't Be Life" came blaring through the speakers. I forgot we were listening to *The Dynasty* when we pulled in the parking lot of the building. I lost it when Scarface said, *"I'm hurting for you dog: but ain't nobody pain is like yours, I just know that heaven'll open these doors."* I felt that shit. I was hurting like hell, but I could only imagine the pain my brother was in knowing that his life was coming to an end.

****

Adonis

Sitting outside of my mother's house, I was trying my hardest to prepare myself for what I had to do. I inhaled a deep breath and held it for a few seconds, then laid my head back on the headrest and tried to figure out the best way to inform her of Lavelle's death; I knew it wouldn't be easy. She wasn't gon' take it too well. I exhaled a long breath, then grabbed Lavelle's hoodie off the backseat and put it on. I looked down at the blood on my shirt, then closed my eyes tightly to fight the tears that were starting to form. I zipped up the hoodie to make sure it covered all the blood, then made my way to my mother's door. I wiped my face and tried to look as natural as I could before ringing the doorbell. I hated to be the one to have to tell my mother that Lavelle was dead, but I wouldn't want her to find out any other way. I heard her yell that she was coming from the other side of the door. I stood tall with a fake smile on my face, trying to mask the pain that I was feeling inside.

"Adonis, don't call yourself pranking me, I ain't got time for that. What do you mean Lavelle's dead? She had her hand on her hip and her face distorted, looking at me like she didn't understand what I was saying, like I was speaking a foreign language or something.

"Ma, he's dead," I reiterated.

Repeating those words made the color disappear from her face, and I could see her heart slowly breaking. I grabbed her and pulled her into my arms. She must have been in shock 'cause she stood in my arms motionless, not returning my embrace. I squeezed her tighter. The muffled sounds of her sobbing vibrated through my chest as her body started heaving heavily. She let out a loud cry as her body slowly fell to the floor.

"NO! NO! NO!" she repeated over and over, shaking her head.

I pulled her closer and held her tighter. I couldn't hold back my own tears any longer. I laid my head on her shoulder and stroked her hair as we both cried. It pained me deeply to see my mother so hurt; my heart ached, and my chest felt like it was about to explode.

I pulled my mother off the floor and sat her on the sofa. She asked if I could make her some tea, and I nodded yes. As I was filling the teapot up with water, I noticed traces of Lavelle's blood on my hand. I stared at it for a minute before washing my hands. After giving my mother her tea, I went upstairs to take a shower. I need to get out of the bloody clothes that I had on.

I stood under the shower, crying and letting the hot water comfort me. I closed my eyes and pictured him lying on the ground dying. My eyes instantly popped open. I ran my hands down my face and started thinking about the shit I seen and learned growing up in a drug-infested neighborhood like I did. Love and loss are two lessons you learn from the start. In this life, if you love something then you better be willing to die for it, because these streets will take that shit in a heartbeat.

It didn't take me too long to figure out that you can't trust a muthafucka out here, and you better watch ya back. Any nigga out here hustling will tell you that this game is all about survival. You win, lose, or die in these streets every day, but a smarter nigga will tell you that if you ain't winning, yo ass is already fuckin' dead. From the moment you start winning and making money, you instantly have a giant target on yo back. A nigga don't care if you just got one more dollar than him; he want all that shit, so you constantly gotta watch out for a jack move at any moment. They coming for yo cash, shiny jewelry, yo car—shit, these thirsty ass niggas will even take the shoes off yo feet.

To survive and win out here in the hood, you had to have balls of steel and a heart of stone. I knew deep down I had both, but there were still lessons I had to learn the hard way. For me, it was tonight. The streets took something from me that they could never give back, my brother. I could still hear the choking sounds he made as I held him and watched his life slip away.

"Why the fuck would they kill my brother?" I whispered.

This fuckin' game would destroy you, no matter who you were. It made mothers bury their kids and take brothers away from brothers. Lavelle had been stolen from me, and my heart felt nothing. Revenge was the only thing on my mind. No one could do revenge better than me. One way or another, I was gon' bury them niggas.

I stepped out of the shower, went into my own room, and grabbed a t-shirt and a pair of jeans out of the closet. Going to the dresser to get some boxer briefs, I noticed blood on my shoes. I grabbed a pair out of the closet and thanked God that I still had clothes there. I placed all the bloody clothes in a duffle bag, then got dressed.

My mother was asleep on the sofa when I came back downstairs. I woke her up and told her that I was leaving. She gave me a hug and kiss.

"Where are you going?" she asked with hoarse voice.

"I have to go see Sieda," I replied.

"Be careful, and tell Sieda that I love her and to call me," she said as she gave me another hug and kiss goodbye.

When I got to Lavelle's door, I could hear music and giggling. Sieda had company, and it seemed like they were having fun. I leaned against the door for a few minutes wondering if I should spoil her fun with this shit. I had no choice. If I didn't tell her now, she would be alone and worried about Lavelle for the rest of the night, and I didn't want to do that to her. I knocked on the door. She opened it with a big grin on her face.

"Adonis." She had a surprised look on her face. "Where's Lavelle?" she asked, looking out of the door.

I stepped inside and closed the door behind me. The expression on her face turned from elated to alarmed.

"Where's Lavelle?" she repeated her question.

"Sieda," I started as my voice cracked.

She took a few steps back, shaking her head no with a horrid look as if she already knew what I was about to tell her. One of her friends turned the music off and they all stared at me with a concerned look.

"Don't tell me that, Adonis," she said as she continued shaking her head no.

"Seida, listen—" I tried to speak again, but she cut me off.

"No Adonis, don't tell me that," she stated with anger, pointing her finger at me.

"Seida, Lavelle is—" I started, and was interrupted by a hard slap to my face.

"I said don't tell me that!" she slapped me again.

As hard as it was for me to say the words, and as bad as my left cheek stung, I had to tell her.

"SIEDA, LAVELLE IS DEAD!" I blurted.

She shook her head no. "I told you not to say that!" she cried out as tears formed in her eyes. She shrieked, then started beating me in the chest with her fist. I wrapped my arms around her and squeezed her tightly.

"NOOOOOO!" she screamed, still trying to hit me. She finally stopped struggling with me and fell into my embrace.

"WHY? WHY? WHY?" she cried.

I felt her body go limp in my arms, then she passed out. I caught her body before she hit the floor, picked her up, and carried her over to the sofa. Her friends started fanning her as I called her name, shaking her. Her friend named Niesha went and got a cold rag to put on her head. She slowly opened her eyes and blinked several times, trying to focus before she tried to sit up.

"Seida, just lay there for a little while," I said, wiping her face and neck with the rag.

"I'm ok, Adonis," she said in a low voice, taking the rag out of my hand. I helped her sit up.

"What happened?" she asked.

"I don't know, I found him shot," I informed her as I fought back my own tears.

"You were there? Who shot him? Where was he? Did he suffer?" she was firing off questions that I really didn't want to answer. "Please Adonis, tell me he didn't suffer." She started crying again. I turned my head to hide the tears that were forming in my eyes.

"Calm down, Sieda, and I will tell you everything I know."

I took her hands in mine and told her everything that I knew, except that he suffered.

Before I left, her friends assured me that they would stay with her for the night so she wouldn't be alone. I thanked them and instructed them to call me if she needed anything. With a heavy heart, I walked back to Lavelle's truck and climbed inside; I was emotionally drained. I checked the time on my watch, and it read 10:18 p.m. I put the key in the ignition and started the engine. I pulled off and headed home, but as I turned onto Suitland Parkway, my mind drifted to Venus and Harmony. I had to go see them, not only to tell Venus about Lavelle, but I needed them. I turned off on Branch Avenue and headed to her house.

Venus

I had just finished making sure that Harmony bathed and put on her pajamas. I put the movie *Frozen* in her DVD player and headed to my bedroom to take a shower. I pinned my hair up and grabbed a few things out of the dresser drawer. The doorbell started ringing.

"Who the hell could that be?" I wondered as I hurried down the steps.

I opened the door, and Adonis was leaning against the wall with his hands in his pockets, one foot on the wall, and his head down.

"What you doing here?" I asked

"I came to see you." He flashed a Kool-Aid smile, then kissed me on the cheek.

He walked into the house and sat on the sofa. I didn't know what it is, but something seemed off. He wasn't walking proudly like normal. His shoulders were more slumped as if something was bothering him.

"Are you ok?" I asked as I sat down beside him.

"Yeah, I'm ok," he answered with a low voice. He sounded kind of hoarse.

"You sure you ok?" I was seeking the truth.

I knew shit had been a little different lately, but I knew Adonis Thompson, and I know that something was wrong. I decided not to push him to talk; I didn't want to make him angry, so I laid my head on his shoulder and told him that I was here whenever he needed to talk. He kissed my head and stroked my hair. We sat in silence for a few minutes, then I heard him sniffle as his breathing became rapid. I turned his head toward mine and stroked his cheek. His eyes were filled with pain as tears formed.

"Adonis, talk to me," I whispered.

His chest started to heave as if he was trying not to cry. Suddenly, he burst into tears. I pulled him into my arms as he let out a loud cry.

"They killed him, they killed my brother. Lavelle's dead," he cried out.

"What?" I asked, just to be clear on what it was he was telling me. He lifted off my shoulder and looked at me with tear pouring outta his eyes.

"Lavelle was killed, he died with his head in my lap." His voice was brittle and low. I couldn't believe what I was hearing.

"NO NO NO! Adonis, this isn't true," I stated, shaking my head in disbelief

"IT IS TRUE, VENUS!" he shouted. "I'll show you," he said as he grabbed my hands and lifted me off of the sofa.

A sharp pain hit me in the chest as we began walking to Lavelle's truck. My breathing faded with each step. Adonis popped the hatchback and pulled out a bag containing bloody clothes.

"See Venus, this is all I have left of my brother, my blood-stained clothes." He sat on the back of the truck, placing the bloody shirt against his chest as he started crying.

I dropped to my knees as I stared at the blood-stained clothes with a horrid look on my face. Covering my face with my hands, I started to cry. The heaviness in my chest and the shaking of my body as I cried caused me to break down. My body slowly tumbled over. Adonis rushed to me in an attempt to catch me before I fall. Wrapping me in his arms, Adonis buried my head in his chest. In the middle of my driveway, me and Adonis cried in each other's arm as we rocked back and forth.

Finally, we got ourselves together and went back inside the house. We both sat on the sofa, staring blankly at nothing at all. The somber mood filled the air as we sat silent, trying to process the fact that Lavelle was dead. I was completely numb, not knowing what to feel. Part of me was mad as hell, but most of me was hurt to the core.

"What happened?" my brittle voice cracked as I spoke.

"I don't know," he answered, shaking his head. "All I know is that he got a call and went to meet somebody; he told me to wait in the car. I heard gunshots and found him shot three times in the chest." He started beating himself in the head with both hands, rocking back and forth while crying. "He died in my arms, Vee; he fuckin' died in my muthafuckin' arms." He was hurt and enraged at the same time. I didn't know what to do or say. I tried to go over what he was saying in my head over and over again.

"Who was he meeting?" I asked.

"I DON'T FUCKIN' KNOW!" he shouted, then his voice got low. "He didn't tell me anything; we pulled up to some fuckin' condemned building and he told me to stay in the car. All I know is he was shot, I found him, he died, and that bitch ass Maurice showed up, then the fuckin' feds. That's it and that's all." He laid his head on the back of the sofa and placed his hands over his face. "My fuckin' brother is dead, Vee; Lavelle is dead." The hard shaking of his body vibrated through the sofa.

Wrapping my arms around his waist, I laid my head on his chest. I felt his arm fall on my back, then his hand ran down my back, stopping on my butt.

"Where's Harmony?" he asked in a whisper.

"She was watching *Frozen*, but she's probably sleep now," I replied. I could almost guarantee she was asleep; normally, as soon as she heard Adonis' voice, she came flying down the steps and into her daddy's arms.

Adonis lifted me up off of his chest, then stood up. He ran his hands down his face, drying his moist face. He let out a sigh as he started walking toward the steps. He looked so lost. His eyes were low, shoulders were slumped, and his head was hanging down. I had never seen him this way, and I was worried. I slid off of the sofa and followed him upstairs to Harmony's room.

He stood in the doorway staring at her as she laid sleeping on her Frozen body pillow. He walked over to her, scooped her up, then put her into bed. He climbed into the bed beside her and wrapped his arms around her. He brushed her hair from her face, kissed her several times on her temple, then buried his head in her back. I stared at them from the doorway for a few minutes, then walked over and kissed them both on the forehead. As I was walking out of the room, Adonis whispered my name. I turned around.

"I love you," he said in a low tone.

I walked back over to the bed and kissed him. I could taste the saltiness of his tears on his lips. He grabbed the back of my head and pulled me deeper into the kiss. As our tongues danced in each other's mouths, I could feel my pearl pulsating and started to get moist. His kisses always made me horny as hell, but the pregnancy hormones had me burning inside like an inferno. My heart started pounding, and I had an insatiable need to be touched. I needed the friction and wasn't gonna be satisfied until I felt his long, thick dick inside of me. Harmony shifted, interrupting our kiss. I was so lost in the moment that I forgot that I was leaning over her. We both snickered, then he laid his head on the top of Harmony's. I left the room and went to my bedroom.

I was sitting on the bed still trying to process everything, Adonis walked in the room and laid across the bed, placing his head in my lap. I started tracing the waves in his hair with my finger.

"SHIT!" he shouted, quickly sitting up. "I didn't call to check on my mother," he said. I picked up the phone and scrolled to her name, then placed the phone on speaker.

"Hello," she answered. Her voice was groggy.

"Hey ma, you sleeping?" I asked.

"Off and on, how are you? Have you talked to Adonis?" she asked.

"I'm right here, ma," he responded, holding the phone up to his mouth so she could hear clearer.

"Baby, how's Sieda? She called me a while ago; she didn't sound so good," she told him.

"I guess as good as expected. She had some friends over and they said they would stay with her, but I'm gon' check on her in the morning," he informed her.

"Ok baby, well call me tomorrow, and Venus," she paused, waiting for me to respond.

"Yes, ma," I answered.

"Take care of him, ok?" she told me.

"I will," I replied. We ended the call. Adonis laid back on the bed, closed his eyes, and started rubbing his temples.

"I have the biggest headache right now," he breathed. "Can I stay here tonight?" he asked.

"What about Raquel, won't she worry?" I responded.

He looked at me side-eyed. "I don't give a fuck," he replied.

"Whatever, Adonis." I shook my head. "You can stay if you want, just try to get some sleep," I added.

"I don't wanna sleep," he said, looking at me with lust-filled eyes.

He rubbed and kissed my stomach, then laid his head on it.

"Baby, daddy gon' handle some business with yo momma; try to chill, aight," he spoke to my stomach.

"What business you got to handle with me?" I asked flirtatiously.

"I had a fucked up emotional day, and I'm about to take my anger and frustrations out on yo pussy—that's what business I got to handle," he answered.

"I didn't say you can fuck. I said you can stay to get some sleep; besides, like you said, you had an emotional day. What you need is to relax, maybe eat, and I will run you some bath water." I cut my eyes at him.

"Man, fuck that; you play too fuckin' much. I know what I need, and right now I need you; besides, you know you want this dick just as bad as I wanna give it to you. Yo ass was wet as fuck when you kissed me. Stop fakin', yo pussy waiting for me to slid up in it," he replied.

"Please, Adonis," I chuckled, waving him away.

"Please, Adonis," he mocked me, tryna imitate my voice. "Yo ass gon' be begging please for real by the time I get done with you," he chuckled.

He slid his hand up my shorts and started touching my box.

"See, just thinking about my dick got yo ass leakin'," he smirked.

I grabbed his hand. "That dick you speak of belongs to Raquel now; and anyway, sex will not ease your pain." I pushed his hand away.

"You got jokes," he laughed as he grabbed my ankles, slid me down onto the bed, and started taking off my shorts.

Even though I didn't agree that sex was what he needed, I knew that if I denied him, he would leave this house and it there was telling what he might do. I'd seen firsthand how Adonis reacted when he wasn't thinking clearly, and with the million thoughts that I knew were going through his head at this moment, he was not thinking rationally. I lifted my ass up so he could pull my shorts off. He took off his t-shirt, then his pants and his rod popped out, already standing at full attention. He climbed between my legs, grabbed my hips, and pulled me upward to his mouth.

"Shit! Adonis, what the fuck?" I squirmed underneath him, already about to nut.

I don't know if this nigga smoked some weed and caught the munchies or what, but he was eating the groceries like he ain't ate in days. He had me clawing at the sheets tryna to get him to ease up some, but the way he had my body positioned perfectly to his mouth, I couldn't get away.

"Adonis, pllleeease," I whined, pleading like I was begging for mercy; truth is, I was.

SLURP! SMACK! SLURP! SMACK!

He was drinking up every single bit of my juices as he stuck two fingers inside of me and started hitting my G-spot. I laid back, closed my eyes, and let him handle his business; shit, I couldn't do anything else. My body was jerking uncontrollably, my heart was racing, and my breathing turned into heavy pants.

"Plllease, wait Adonis, oh my goodness, pllllleeeeasse." My head was spinning and I started feeling dizzy. I don't know what he was doing to me, but I was feeling drunk.

"AAAAhhhh!" I let out a loud scream as I had the biggest orgasm ever.

"Told you that you was gonna be begging," he smirked, licking my juices off his lips.

In one swift motion, Adonis flipped me over and put me on all fours.

"MMMMM," I moaned. I arched my back so he could go deeper. Adonis grabbed my hips and stroked me hard and deep. I was trying my hardest not to tap out, but I couldn't help it any longer. I reached back and tapped his arm.

"Oh, first you begging, now you tappin' out; nah, you mine tonight," he said as he pounded and thrust deep inside my walls, making me feel every inch of his thickness.

He pinned my arms behind my back with one hand, then grabbed my hair with the other as he continued plowing deep inside of me. The painful pleasure he was giving me had my pussy muscles tightening, sending a tingling sensation through my body.

"Shit, Adonis," I breathed as my body bounced off and on his pole, causing my kitty to pulsate. I felt like I was about to explode.

Adonis always had a way of bringing me to a quick nut, and my kitty loved to erupt on his pole. Tonight, as he dealt with his pain by taking all of his frustrations out on my pussy, something felt different. Suddenly, without breaking his stroke and after beating my shit up from the back, Adonis let go of my hair and arms. He hovered over my back and slowed down his pace. Flipping me over and wrapping my legs around his waist, he looked deep into my eyes as if he was trying to penetrate my soul. I may not have experienced this type of loss, but I was able to see his pain.

As he stared intensely into my eyes, it was as if he wanted to speak, but no words needed to be spoken. The glossiness that covered his eyes told me that in this moment, he needed me and didn't want me to ever leave him. I began to slowly gyrate my hips and brought him closer to me. I held him close as we both inhaled each other's scent. Pumping in and out of me, we turned a quick fucking session into a deep, passionate love making sessions. Our hearts became one and our souls were forever tangled. He was mine and I was his. After our final release of the night, we held each other until sleep found us.

One week later

Adonis

Today is the day where we are laying my brother to rest. No matter how well I thought I was prepared, nothing could prepare me for that long walk from the limo to the front of the church, where Lavelle was now at rest. As he lay in his grey suit with a blue and grey tie, my eyes scanned his casket and my heart began to sink. Being inside this huge church with cathedral ceilings seemed small as I felt the walls closing in on me. The soulful melody coming from the organ filled the church as the singer made her way to the mic. I closed my eyes and let the music transport me to a place of joy. I opened my eyes as the singer started singing her own version of "All My Tears" by Julie Miler. I look at my mother; her long black dress swept across her ankles as she nervously bounced her knee. I placed my hand over hers to cease the movement. She looked at me as a single tear overflowed her puffy eyes and slowly rolled down her moist cheek. My heart broke even more, then I looked over at Sieda; she was staring blankly at Lavelle's casket with bloodshot eyes. Sieda started sobbing, and Debora, her mother placed an arm around Sieda's neck laying her head on her shoulder.

I blinked rapidly, struggling to hold back the tears that were forming in my eyes. The emptiness that I was feeling staring at the cherry wood casket containing my brother's body was unbearable. I wished he was sitting next to me. I would give anything just to see his smiling face, or hear his deep voice giving one of his lectures that I hated. I swallowed, trying to make the huge lump in my throat disappear, but no matter how hard I swallowed, the lump wouldn't budge. I glanced around the church looking at the many grieving faces that gathered together to mourn my brother's death.

I saw Mrs. Hailey, one of our childhood neighbors; she was wiping away her tears with a tissue. I thought of the day me and Lavelle got in trouble for turning on the fire hydrant in front of her house. It was hot as hell that day and we was tryna find relief. We got a wrench from my father's tool box, turned the hydrant on, and started playing in the water. Mrs. Hailey was so angry; she grabbed us by the ears and dragged us all the way home. My mother whipped our asses.

"What I tell y'all about running around here actin' like Bebe kids, got folks bringing y'all home like y'all ain't got no damn home training!" my mother ranted as she stormed into her room to get her thick leather ass whippin' belt.

Chuckling to myself at that thought, I continued to scan the room. Shariff, the prison-made Muslim as me and Lavelle called him, did five years in the D.C. Central for selling drugs. He came home a Muslim telling us how we were pushing poison into the black community. Me and Lavelle would listen to him talk, then laugh at his fake Muslim ass. How in the hell you say to us, "y'all niggas poisoning y'all bodies with that swine, " but secretly fucking up pork chop sandwiches like it ain't nothing? I shook my head.

Mr. Li was sitting in one of the rows toward the back of the church. He noticed me and nodded his head. I smiled and nodded back. I was swept with an overwhelming feeling of love as my eyes continued roaming the church. I knew my brother was loved and respected, but I never imagined that he touched so many lives.

My eyes darted slightly to the right and I locked eyes with Frank. His face was emotionless, but his eyes held the same pain as mine. That shit didn't faze me, though; he was the reason why we were here in the first place. I could feel my blood begin to boil as the love I was feeling looking around the room quickly transformed into anger. As

I continued my death stare at Frank, I noticed a nigga sitting a couple of rows behind him; he was wearing a black brim hat that covered his face. I didn't know what it was about the mysterious man, but there was something about him that felt real familiar. I felt his eyes peering at me even though I couldn't see them. It seemed like his presence was known only to me. He slowly shook his head no as if he was telling me not to do something as he sat with authority looking straight forward. I took one last glance at Frank, and the scowl I had on my face returned. I quickly turned my head to suppress my anger.

I glanced at Venus, who was staring at me and as if she was reading my mind, she mouthed, "This is not the time, calm down." She rubbed her stomach to remind me of my seed that was growing inside.

Nodding my head, I slowly blinked my eyes, letting her know that I agreed with her words. I placed my head in my hands, breathing into them as I turned my attention to the countless people who were speaking about my brother's character and offering their condolences. I heard the speaker say the two words that usually meant a lot: I'm sorry. Those words don't mean shit to me no more.

A hush fell over the crowd as we waited for the next speaker to approach the podium. The sound of him clearing his throat caught my attention.

"Good morning everyone," a familiar voice spoke.

I looked up. That's when I saw him, the nigga that walked out of our lives with no looking back. I hadn't laid eyes on that nigga since that day.

"My name is Levar Thompson, Lavelle's father." As soon as he spoke those words, my anger returned.

I could feel my blood boiling as I anxiously bounced my knee, fighting the urge to snatch his ass off the pulpit, drag his ass outta the church, and beat the fuck outta his sorry ass. Raquel grabbed my knee tryna stop it from shaking. I knew she called herself being there for me, but I didn't give a fuck. My anger turned to rage. I gave her the evil eye.

"You're only sitting here because you have my child...but real talk, that's not your seat," I murmured, pushing her hand from my knee.

She placed her hands in her lap, interlocking her fingers as she sat frozen and looked straight forward as if she was scared to move. This bitch didn't understand; Venus was the only woman I wanted sitting next to me. She was the only woman I loved. I glanced at Venus as Levar continued speaking.

"My life changed the moment Lavelle was born. I looked into his eyes and all my troubles disappeared. He was my firstborn, my life. He was more than a son; he was my reason for my existence."

"I can't listen to this bullshit," I said in a low voice as I got up and stormed out of the church.

I was standing under the huge oak tree tryna get some air to calm myself down. *How in the fuck could this nigga stand up there and lie?* I thought as I loosened my tie. This piece of shit ass nigga spoke about my brother like he actually knew who he was, like he was actually in our lives. I let out a sigh and a yell as I threw my tie on the ground.

"I guess he wants a fuckin' father of the year award now, fuckin' no good ass bastard," I said as I leaned against the tree.

I heard the rustling of the grass, alerting me that someone was approaching. I turned around and came face to face with the love of my life, Venus. She had a worried expression on her face as she walked toward me and with no words spoken; she wrapped her arms around my waist. I kissed the top of her head and buried her head in my chest. I felt a hand on my shoulder.

"Son, can we talk?" Levar asked.

"Get yo hands off me," I responded through clenched teeth as I snatched my shoulder away from him. "I'm not yo fuckin' son," I added.

"Adonis, please hear him out," my mother pleaded, but her plea fell on deaf ears. I wasn't tryna hear shit this nigga had to say.

"Look, Adonis, I love you and Lavelle."

"If my brother's name come outta yo mouth one more time, I swear I'll kill you where you stand," I warned him. My mother called my name again tryna to get my attention, but I ignored her.

"You walked outta our lives and never looked back; now you wanna come here playin' daddy and shit," I continued.

"Let's get this straight right now, Adonis; you can hate me all you want, but you will not disrespect me, you understand?" He walked up on me with his chest poking out like he put fear in a nigga or something.

"Understand this, my brother is dead because of you and your actions; this is your fault. His blood is on yo hands; I have no respect for you." My tone was sadistic, and so was the look I was giving him as I stepped to him with my chest poked out the same way he stepped to me.

"Now wait a minute, Lavelle—"

As soon as he spoke his name, I grabbed him by the throat and pinned him to the tree.

"I told you not to say his name again," I said through clenched teeth as I tightened my grip around his neck. I was tryna choke the life outta his trifling ass. My mother and Venus were struggling to pull me off of him, but my grip was so tight that they couldn't move me.

"Adonis, turn him loose."

I heard the sweet, angelic sound of Grandma Thompson's voice speaking to me with authority. She appeared outta nowhere; I didn't notice her in the church when I was looking around at all the people that were attending. Audrey Thompson, my father's mother, was the one person in my father's family that stayed in me and Lavelle's lives. She lived in Chicago and would send for us to spend summers with her. My father didn't even know that we were staying with her. As we got older, we stopped staying summers with her, but we always made sure to visit her a few times a year. She placed her hand on my shoulder, tapping it lightly as if she was telling me that she understood my pain. I let him go and she pulled me into a loving embrace, just like she did when I was a child.

"He's still your father," she said in a soft-spoken voice.

I pulled away from her grip. "No disrespect Grandma, but he don't exist to me." I pointed at my father, who was still doubled over tryna catch his breath.

I walked off and got into the back of the limo as all my emotions came to the surface. I felt like I was suffocating. I unbuttoned the top two buttons of my shirt and let out a deep breath. Venus slid into the limo beside me and pulled me into her arms. I burst into tears. A few minutes later, Raquel and my mother joined us in the limo.

"Adonis, baby," my mother said in a low tone, placing her hand on my knee.

"Mrs. Thompson, please give him a minute," Venus insisted before my mother could say another word.

"I think I can handle my man," Raquel said with an attitude.

"She got this," my mother told her, tapping her on the knee.

"I'm carrying his baby, don't you think I can take care of him?" she asked, staring at Venus.

I felt Venus tighten her grip around my neck as her breathing became heavy. She was pissed, and so was I. This was not the way I wanted her to find out about Raquel's pregnancy. I could have jumped out of that seat and choked the shit outta Raquel; that bitch knew exactly what she was doing. I pulled away from Venus, trying to sit up; she tightened the hold she had on me so that I couldn't move. I knew her evil ass wanted to fuck me up one way or another; my ass was grass—no ifs, ands, or buts about it.

At the burial, everyone stood silently with their heads down as the preacher said his final prayer, but not me. My eyes were glued to Frank and Maurice. They took something that I loved from me; it was only right that I took something they loved: their empire and their lives.

"Ashes to ashes, dust to dust."

The preacher made a cross motion over Lavelle's casket as they started lowering it into the ground. Venus grabbed my hand and laid her head on my shoulder. I kissed her forehead as I watched my brother stop at his final resting place.

The repast was at my mother's house, so it was swarming with tons of family and friends. Some were talking amongst themselves tryna catch up, some were getting acquainted with people that they didn't know, and some were telling stories about Lavelle. I was sitting on the sofa listening to the chatter. Some of the stories were funny, some were about the nice things he did for people, but the ones that tugged on my heart were the ones about him always fussing. As painful as it was to hear those stories, I had to laugh. It seemed like Lavelle had to have something to fuss about at least once a day. It could be something as simple as things being out of place or something major, like not finding out who hit the traps; it didn't matter.

Adonis, nigga why you sitting over here looking all fucked up and shit? Fuck wrong with you? I heard Lavelle's voice in my head having one of his rants.

I laughed to myself 'cause I could picture him standing over top of me with his face scrunched up saying those exact words to me. I took a deep breath and exhaled it, trying to ease my mind. Thinking about Lavelle was too painful for me. I needed a break from the crowd of people and their stories. I excused myself, got up, and headed to the back yard. I sat on the outdoor sofa that set in the middle of my mother's garden, surrounded by a beautiful array of colors. I could feel my body starting to relax. I took in a deep breath to inhale the scent of the flowers.

As I scanned the garden, my eyes were drawn to a bush of Dahlia flowers. Hoping that my mother didn't find out, I picked one and started twirling it. I watched as the bright pink and yellow colors danced around in my hands. A small smile grew on my face.

There was something about how the yellow peeked from the center of the bright pink flower that made me feel warm inside. Curious to find out what it smelled like, I put it to my nose and took a sniff. I was expecting the flower to have a sweet smell, but I was wrong. This flower had no smell at all; I was shocked.

"How could a flower as beautiful as this one have no smell?" I asked myself as I placed the flower to my nose and sniffed it again.

"You better hide that before your mother see it; you know she gon' kick yo ass," Venus laughed as she approached me.

I laughed and placed the flower in the middle of the bush. Venus sat down beside me, crossing her right leg over her left; she leaned against the arm of the sofa and gave me a questioning look.

"Too much for you, huh?" she asked, already knowing the answer.

Letting out a sigh, I laid my head back against the sofa and rubbed my hands down my face.

"How the fuck am I gon' do this, Venus?" I asked.

"It won't be easy, but you will get through this," she assured, taking my hand in hers and rubbing it with her thumb.

"Why are you here consoling me right now? I mean, with what happened in the limo," I kissed her hand.

"Adonis, we will talk about that later. This is not the time or place to have this conversation. All I am worried about is you," she spoke in a comforting tone.

I peeped at her out the corner of my eyes and smiled. Not too many women would want to be by my side after finding out that another woman was pregnant at the same time as her, but Venus was not like all women; she put her own feelings aside to be supportive. I just realized that was what she'd been doing our entire relationship. I got it now.

"Boy, wipe that damn smile off your face. This conversation will definitely not be something to smile about," she said, crossing her arms around her stomach as she rolled her eyes.

I ran my fingers through her hair, tugging lightly on a curl to straighten it, then letting it go so it could snap back into place like a spring.

"How my baby doing?" I asked.

"The baby is fine," she replied, rubbing her stomach.

"I'm not talking about that baby," I chuckled a little.

"Harmony's fine too, she's with her Aunt Layna," she stated.

"I'm not talking about Harmony either."

I turned her head and stroked her cheek lightly as I gazed deeply into her eyes. I brushed her hair from her face. She sucked her bottom lip into her mouth, biting down on it as she closed her eyes tightly like she was fighting back tears.

"I'm good on the outside, but an emotional wreck on the inside," she spoke in a quiet tone as I continued caressing her cheek.

A single tear rolled down her cheek. I don't know if she was crying for Lavelle or because of all the pain I'd been causing her lately, but that tear sent a shooting pain straight through my heart, making me feel fucked up. I moved closer to her. I wiped the tear from her eye, then slid my finger down the side of her face to her chin. Lifting her chin, I planted a soft kiss on her lips.

Raquel

I was standing in the doorway of the back yard watching how affectionate Adonis was with Venus. They were sitting outside near the garden talking. He stroked her hair while gazing lovingly into her eyes. I could feel the jealousy grow when I saw how tenderly he kissed her. He never handled me with such gentleness, and watching him with her had me enraged. This bitch was becoming a serious thorn in my side. She'd been up in his face all day, and I was not having it anymore. I worked hard to get Adonis, and I'd be damned if some stupid ass ex of his was gonna take him away. The bitch had her chance.

I was tired of fuckin' around with these fake ass hustlas out here acting like they had long pockets. They be in the clubs poppin' bottles and making it rain, promising to take me out of the strip club. I found out how empty those promises and their pockets were after we fucked. These niggas was broker than me; how in the hell they was gonna get me off that pole? Adonis was different, though; he actually had the money that he was spending. I worked at Illicit Dream, Frank's strip club. I was the one they called Fantasy. I would dress in costumes that fit a fantasy girl that men would love to be with. I always wore a mask to keep an element of mystery about me. I paid attention to the men that came in and out of the club, looking for someone to get my hooks into.

Lavelle was the first to spark my interest. I used to see him coming in and out of Frank's office, so I knew he was one of the heads. I asked the other girls about him, and they told me that he was in a committed relationship and would never cheat. Usually, I wouldn't care about all that, but I didn't want the drama. Then one day, I was standing on the side of the building smoking a blunt before working. I saw him talking to Adonis at the car. He went into the building, and Adonis sat outside and waited. I overheard him on the phone asking someone if they got the information he wanted. He spoke in a manner that let me know that he was a man of importance, a man with some authority. I made him my mark. I was determined to find out all I need to know about him. Lucky for me, I ran into him at the liquor store a week later, and from then on I did what I had to do to make him mine. He came into the club to chill sometimes, and I made it my business to give him a lap dance so vicious that the nigga's dick would be on swole, and he was ready to fuck. If Frank's ass wasn't clocking how many niggas we took in the back or lap dances, I would have let him. Thank God, he never found out that I was Fantasy from Illicit Dream.

If this bitch think she gonna come crawl her way back to him, she got me fucked up, I thought as I marched down the steps.

The clicking sound that my heels made on the steps was so loud that I thought they were gonna turn around and notice how pissed off I was. I stopped to calm myself; I was not gonna let this bitch see me sweat.

"Hey, baby, I been looking all over for you," I said in a pleasant voice, wearing a fake ass grin.

I tried giving him a kiss, but he moved his head slightly to the left so I ended up kissing his cheek. Venus folded her lips in her mouth as if she was tryna hide a smile. I gave her a hateful look, and she had the nerve to snicker.

"Well, Adonis, your boo here now, so I'm going inside to check on MA," she stated in a sarcastic tone, putting the emphasis on *ma* as she patted his hand.

I rolled my eyes as I watched her sashay her ass into the house. I tried to sit on Adonis' lap, but he slid to the other end of the sofa.

"So, what's going on, why you acting so standoffish?" I asked, sitting on the sofa beside him.

"Raquel, leave me alone. I'm not in the mood to talk to you right now," he said in a low voice.

"Adonis, I know today is a real fucked up day for you, but you don't have to treat me like this." I reached for his hand, and he snatched it away.

"RAQUEL, LEAVE ME THE FUCK ALONE!" he shouted.

"So, I can't even touch you? What the fuck did I do?" I questioned with an attitude.

"First, Raquel, watch yo fuckin' mouth when you talk to me. You know what this is between me and you; stop tryna turn it into something it's not. Stop tryna act like you don't know that I am only staying with you because you don't have nowhere else to go," he replied.

"It's because of her? You don't wanna show me any attention around her." My voice was brittle as I spoke.

"Do I ever show you attention? You were a bed warmer who just ended up pregnant. If I don't show you attention, it's because I don't want to." I could hear the seriousness in his tone as well as see it in his eyes.

"But you still fuck me, though," I pointed out. He laughed.

"You still in my bed, right?" he asked with raised brows. I didn't respond. "Look, let's make this clear for the last time. I'm only tolerating yo ass because you carrying my seed and don't have nowhere to go; that night when I came home, I was gon' tell you to leave, but you hit me with this pregnancy shit," he paused, then looked at me with a questioning look.

"Speaking of that, what was that shit in the limo?" he asked with a hateful look on his face.

"I just thought that Venus should know the truth," I smirked.

"The truth?" he laughed "Never mind, don't answer that. Go home, Raquel; I will deal with you later," he said slightly above a whisper.

"Why, so your baby momma can be all up in yo face? Fuck that," I chuckled as I crossed my legs and folded my arms. "She needs to know that I'm having your baby, and I'm not going anywhere," I laughed. He jumped up and quickly snatched me up by my arm.

"You think this shit funny, you got jokes? Well, here's a joke for yo ass, she's carrying my baby too. The difference is, I want hers—not yours." He spat those words at me like venom. "I don't see you laughing now," he smirked.

"FUCK YOU, ADONIS!" I shouted as I stormed away.

****

I was sitting at home on the sofa pissed the hell off. I couldn't believe Adonis was treating me so badly. I knew he'd been a little fucked up ever since I told him that I was pregnant, and had been treating me like shit, but not like he was today. Today, he was just plain ole surly. Feeling my anger rise, I quickly wiped away my tears. I wasn't gonna waste no muthafuckin' tears on a nigga that didn't give a fuck about me, but what he needed to know and understand was that I wasn't going nowhere, and neither was my baby; fuck him and that thirsty ass bitch he was pressed for.

I hurried upstairs to his bedroom and snatched a couple of armfuls of clothes out of his closet, then I grabbed some of his most expensive shoes. I throw them all in the bathtub and pour bleach all over them.

"Yeah nigga, that's why I'm bleaching your shit. Talkin' bout you don't want my baby, nigga FUCK YOU. I'll make sure yo ass never be happy. I can be a miserable bitch and make yo life miserable as shit. I promise if you leave me for that bitch, I will make yo life a living hell," I fume as I empty the second bottle of bleach on his shit.

The smell from the bleach made me cough. I hurried out of the bathroom and closed the door. I sat on his bed thinking; I needed to get Venus out of the way. I picked up the phone and made a call.

"What's good?"

"Look, this shit ain't working as planned; we need a plan B just in case."

"Ok, what do you have in mind?"

"First, I need to get the baby mother out of the way."

Adonis

I was still sitting in the garden trying to wrap my head around everything that transpired today; still couldn't believe my brother was gone. I laid my head back and closed my eyes. I took in breaths, tryna let the fresh air relax me.

"Adonis," I heard my grandma Thompson call my name.

I turned around and noticed a beautiful dark-skinned young lady with shoulder-length jet black hair like mine, walking toward me with my grandma. She looked to be no older than 18. I stood up and met my grandmother halfway. I greeted her with a hug and a kiss on the cheek.

"It's good to see you, Grandma," I said as I held her hand and led her over to the sofa.

"Adonis, I would like for you to meet someone. This is gonna come as a shock to you." She took my hand in hers. "Adonis, this is your sister, Sabrinae." I had to make sure I understood what she said.

"My sister?" I repeated with a puzzled look.

"Yes, Adonis. I am your sister. Levar is my father," she stated with a sweet, silvery voice.

To say I was shocked is an understatement. I opened and closed my mouth trying to find the words to say, but nothing would come out. Sabrinae took my hand.

"It's nice to meet you, big bro," she chuckled as she shook my hand.

"I-i-it's nice to, mmm, meet you too," I stuttered, still trying to articulate my words.

"Your fath...I mean Levar wanted to introduce you to her himself, but well, you know," my grandmother told me.

This was unreal to me, but the more I studied her face, the more I knew it was real. She looked like a mixture of me and Lavelle. She had my smooth, dark skin tone, jet black wavy hair, and brown eye color. She had Lavelle's facial features, which was understandable. I was dark like my father and had his dark hair, but I looked like my mother. Lavelle was opposite; he looked just like my father. He had all his features, including his dark hair, but he had my mother's peanut butter skin tone, and we both inherited her light brown eyes.

"I wish we could have met under different circumstance, and I would have at least gotten to meet Lavelle," she said with a huge smile on her face. I nodded my head, still shocked.

"Look, I know this is kind of crazy, but—" Sabrinae started.

"Kind of?" I cut her off, looking at her with a scrunched face.

"Adonis, hear her out," my grandmother demanded.

"I'm sorry, I can't right now, Grandma. I got to get outta here, excuse me." I hurried away, leaving my grandmother and sister behind calling my name.

It was just too damn much for me to handle. I rushed through the back door and bumped into my mother.

"I see you met Sabrinae," she said in a cheerful voice, wearing a big ass grin on her face.

"You knew?" I asked in disbelief.

I didn't understand how my mother would let me be blindsided like that; first, seeing that nigga at the funeral, then he brings a sister I never knew I had. I was hurt, angry, and confused all at once. She confirmed that she knew for a while; the day I popped up over her house, Lavar and Sabrinae was there tryna figure out the best way for him to introduce our sister to us, and the best way for him to try to build a relationship. Fuck that, I didn't want a relationship with him—ever. I was at a loss for words and needed space. Without saying a word, I brushed past my mother and rushed out the front door.

"Adonis! Adonis, wait up," Venus called from behind as she ran toward me.

"Are you alright?" she asked once she caught up with me.

"You shouldn't be running in your condition." I grabbed her around her waist and walked her to the car.

"Don't worry about me, I got this. Now, let's go for a ride," she suggested.

"Venus, I'm not going for a ride, I'm leaving," I stated.

"No, you are getting in the car and we are going for a ride." She tilted her head to the side while she curled her lips, raised her brows, and folded her arms.

Looking at her, I knew that protesting would only lead to an argument, and I wasn't in the mood to argue with her. She nudged me with her shoulder as she walked past me and got into the passenger side of the car. I chuckled, then slid into the car and put the key in the ignition.

"You don't run shit, bossy," I playfully mushed her head.

"Just shut up and drive," she giggled.

The car was silent as we drove through the city. I was going over everything in my head and Venus was staring at me, wanting to say something.

"What you got to say, Venus?" I asked as I turned into Tanglewood Community Park. I parked my car in the designated area and shut off the engine. I unlatched my seatbelt, then turned to face Venus.

"Well?" I questioned with raised brows.

"Oh, I have a lot to say. I'm just trying to decide if I want to say it or not," she stated.

"Man, stop playing games and say what the fuck you want," I snapped.

"Ok, so when did you plan on telling me that you were gonna be a daddy?" she asked in a sarcastic tone. "Don't get me wrong, I understand everything happened so fast, but I don't deserve to find out the way I did," she continued.

"You're right and honestly, I was tryna find the right time to tell you." I took her hands in mine. "I'm sorry," I added.

"The right time would have been when you found out, assuming that you didn't already know when we found out I was pregnant." She pulled her hands out of mine, giving me a questioning look.

"No, I didn't know. In fact, I found out the same day when I went home to tell her that it was over," I told her the truth, hoping that she would let the conversation go.

"So, I take it you didn't break up with her 'cause you had the bitch on your arm today, riding in the limo and shit, taking her rightful place as your woman."

She started to get out of the car, but I grabbed her arm. She snatched away, got out of the car, and stormed off. I hurried outta the car, running behind her. I caught up to her and grabbed her arm. She turned around and started swinging on me. I grabbed her by her wrist to stop her.

"Baby, listen to me; she would never be my woman, I love you," I said with a pleading look, hoping that she believed me.

"But you keep hurting me." Her voice was small as she spoke. "You think I'm gonna be with you, and that bitch is having your baby too?" she asked. Her eyes were narrowed, but I could still see the pain inside of them.

My heart ached and all I wanted to do was hold her and tell her that everything would be ok, but the truth was, I wasn't really sure that it would be.

"Venus, I can't do this shit today." She looked at me as if she was shooting daggers at me.

"Oh, trust me, I had no intentions of doing this shit today either, but fuck it. I can't keep holding this shit in. I know shit been fucked up for you, but what you seem to not get in yo got damn head is that every muthafucking thing been fucked up for me too. I lost you, we broke up, I also lost the man who I came to love and considered my brother as well. The last conversation we had, you said that you was coming correct, gonna do this shit right, you said you was coming back to me. Now, all that shit is shot to hell, I'm having another baby by the man that I love, and I can't be happy 'cause he got another bitch knocked the fuck up, and at the end of the fuckin' day when you go home, you going home to her and all I have to go home to is a broken heart that you created. So you wanna talk about you can't do this shit today? Well nigga, I can't do this shit today or any other fuckin' day, period. I'm done." She stormed off.

Venus

I'm sitting on the bench, trying to figure out what the hell just happened, I really didn't mean to bring any of that shit up today, but it was hard as hell not to. How much more shit did I have to take from his ass? I kept taking blow after blow; it was like his bullshit never ended. I hated that I loved him so much; shit would be so much easier if I didn't. I crossed my legs and rested my elbow on my knee, then I rested my chin on my hand and stared at the children playing on the playground. I saw this one little girl; she was dark-skinned with long, curl ponytails, sliding down the slide and into her father's arms. She had the biggest, brightest grin on her face like she was the happiest little girl in the world. Her father picked her up and twirled around with her in his arms, and she was giggling. I started grinning myself; they reminded me of Adonis and Harmony. Their father-daughter bond started when Harmony was in the womb. She would be still all day, no kicking or flipping, nothing; but as soon as

Adonis start talking, she would start kicking the shit out of me like she was playing soccer. I smiled at the little girl and her father.

"Can we talk?" Adonis asked as he approached the bench.

I sat back against the bench, folding my arms and crossing my legs. I really didn't see a point in talking anymore. I said all that I had to say.

"Adonis, it's really no need to talk," I said.

"Just hear me out." He sat on the bench beside me and placed his arm around the back of the bench.

I turned toward him, giving him my full attention. "Ok, go 'head, talk."

"I didn't know how bad I was hurting you, I'm sorry." His voice was remorseful. I could tell that his apology was sincere.

"I fucked up, I know. I thought that I was supporting you enough, but I get it now. I wasn't giving you the type of support that you needed, and this whole Raquel thing went too far too fast. I met her when we wasn't fuckin' around; we were in the liquor store, and she was basically throwing pussy at me."

I shifted in my seat, not really wanting to hear the details of their relationship, but I let him continue.

"I was only supposed to hit and quit, but she kept coming back and staying the night, I hated sleeping alone, so I allowed it to happen. I missed holding you in my sleep. I was lonely, and when she was there, I wasn't lonely anymore. Venus, I love you and I want to be with you. I can go home now and kick her ass out; just tell me we have a chance, tell me you will give me the opportunity to make things right between us," he pleaded.

As much as I wanted to say yes, I couldn't; not with Raquel having his baby. Besides, I didn't like the bitch, but I wouldn't let him leave her alone and pregnant. I took his face in my hands.

Looking deep into his eyes, I said, "Don't do that, Adonis; she needs you right now."

"So do you, and I need you too." He grabbed my hands from his face, cupped them in his hands, then placed them on his chest.

"First, it's not about your needs and secondly, I don't need you anymore. I'm fine on my own," I assured. "Look, Adonis, maybe our time is over, and I'm cool with that. I just want to live my life and be happy."

"Venus, our time is not over, but I will let you live and be happy. I won't give up on us, though." He got up and headed toward the car.

I stared out of the window as we drove back to Adonis' mother's house. I was captivated by the beautiful trees blowing in the breeze. I was imagining how I would feel if I could be as free as the trees; free from all the nonsense, and all of the pain. I didn't fully understand how me and Adonis got to this place. I only needed to get myself together, get my career started, and do something on my own that I could be proud of. I put my life on hold and watched him grow as a man, coming into his own. I felt that it was time for me to become the woman I dreamed of being. Maybe it was selfish of me to want to do things on my own, to have my own. I was so dependent on him, and I started to feel worthless. I wished he could have understood what I needed, or maybe I didn't consider his feelings in my decision making.

I glanced over at Adonis; he had a stern look on his face, as if he was deep in thought. His jaws were clenched tightly, and his brows were furrowed as he stared straight at the road. I turned my head back around and continued looking out of the window, and started wondering what would have happened if I didn't leave; maybe this whole situation was my fault. I snickered to myself thinking Kay Kay would kick my ass if she knew that I was questioning my decisions. She felt that I did exactly what I needed to do, and that Adonis was the blame for everything. I really didn't know.

"Baby, I promise, we gon' be aight," Adonis spoke in a low voice, reaching across the center console and placing his hand on top of mine as he squeezed it.

I could see all the love that he held for me in his gaze, but for me, love wasn't enough. I removed my hand from his and placed my hands in my lap. He stared at me for a quick second, then turned his attention back to the road.

We arrived at his mother's house 15 minutes later. I hurried out of the car and into the house, leaving Adonis sitting in the driveway. I immediately started cleaning up the kitchen. I was standing at the sink rinsing leftover residue off of the plates, preparing them for the dishwasher. Adonis came up behind me and placed his arms around me, grabbing the counter and pinning me against the sink.

"I meant what I said, Venus; we ain't over." He moved my hair to the other side and planted a soft wet kiss on my neck before walking away.

After everyone left, I finished cleaning the house, then went upstairs to check on Harmony. She was in the guestroom sleeping peacefully. I stood in the doorway watching my baby girl curled up, looking just like her father. I walked over to her and pulled the covers up, then kissed her on the cheek. I left the room, cracking the door behind me. I went to the bathroom in Adonis' old room and turned the water on in the tub. I poured my chamomile and vanilla bubble bath into the water. I went into the room and gathered my towel and robe, then headed back to the bathroom to take a nice relaxing bubble bath. Sitting in the tub and letting the aroma from the bubble bath soothe me, my emotions took over and I wept. I covered my face with my hands and bent over as everything I was holding in for so long came to surface. I broke down.

Finally, regaining composure, I added more hot water to my bath, then washed my body. My mind was clouded as I dried myself and headed into the bedroom. I sat on the bed looking around the room. I started reflecting back to the beginning of me and Adonis' relationship. I noticed a picture on the wall next to the mirror. I went over and took the picture off of the wall. I looked at it and smiled. It was a picture that Lavelle took of us at his house on the day Adonis told me that he loved me for the first time. I went back over to the bed and sat back down, still staring down at the picture.

"I wonder if it was possible for us to ever completely go back to that place," I whispered to myself as I took a trip down memory lane.

I laid back on the bed, placed my hands behind my head, and thought about the early years of our relationship. I turned on my side, grabbed a pillow, and buried my face into it. I let out a sigh, trying to relieve the heaviness in my chest that was causing a lump to rise in my throat.

"God, I love him so much," I bawled as I shed tears.

TAP! TAP! TAP! TAP!

The light tapping on the door caught my attention. I used my robe to wipe away my tears.

"Come in," I called out.

Mrs. Thompson slowly opened the door and peeked in. I asked if she needed anything. She shook her head no, then came and sat beside me. She placed her arm around my neck and pulled me to her chest, then placed her other arm around me and stroked my hair. For some reason, her embrace brought back my emotions. I wrapped my arms around her waist, burying my head deeper into her chest. My breathing became labored as I sobbed into her bosom.

"Everything will work itself out, baby. I promise," she assured.

Although she spoke in a pleasant tone, her voice still trembled with emotion with every word.

"Does this get any easier?" I asked as she dabbed my face with a tissue.

"I would be lying if I tell you that heartbreak becomes easier with time; every hurt is different, just like love." She raised my head and brushed my hair away from my face. "Love is easy; you just have to learn that it's ok to be selfish at times," she continued.

"What you mean, ma?" I asked, confused.

"I said what I meant; it's ok to be selfish. You needed something for yourself; you did the right thing by getting what you need the best way you could. It's ok to demand help from your man, and it's ok to demand respect from anyone. Don't feel like you did anything out of the norm." She kissed my forehead. "And baby, it's ok to take your man back," she added.

"Wait, what?" I looked at her with a scrunched face, wondering why would she say that.

"Venus, Adonis is your man; so what that bitch is pregnant, you are too. You have every right to have your children in the same household as their father. You are the one he loves and needs. The truth is, you love and need him just as much. So, if you want your man, go get him; fuck that hoe."

"Ma, don't call the girl a hoe," I chuckled.

"I call people like I see them. You can play all nice and polite if you want, but you and I both know that little sneaky bitch is a hoe; shit, who knows if that's my son's baby she carrying? I don't want that trifling hussy as my daughter in law; as far as I'm concerned, my daughter is sitting right here— regardless of anything, you will always be my daughter." She tapped my leg, then stood up.

"Maybe I'm being selfish, but hell; that's ok." She shrugged her shoulders and smirked, kissed me on my forehead, then left out of the room.

"I love that woman," I whispered as I picked up the phone to call Kay Kay.

Kay Kay

"Fuck, Loco," I moaned, rubbing my hands through his dreads.

He had my legs pushed back into my chest and spread open, using his fingers to hold my pussy lips open while he was face deep in my kitty. He was slowly circling around my clit with his tongue while sucking it lightly.

"Damn baby, yo pussy always taste so fuckin' good," he said in a low, lust-filled voice.

The shit felt so good; I had to raise up on my elbows and give him a look that said *you eating the shit outta this pussy*. I started gyrating my hips while watching him devour my kitty. I felt light tingling sensations go through my body to the top of my head. My eyes closed tightly as my body started shivering. I let my head fall back as I thrusted my pelvis to match his rhythm.

"Loco baby, stop playing and make me cum," I breathed, speeding up my pace.

He grabbed my hips and pulled me downward, then licked me repeatedly from my asshole to clit, stopping for a few seconds to suck on my bud. His tongue made its way back to the back hole, flicking in and out while he used his index finger and pointer to fondle my bud; he used his other hand to stick his fingers inside my hole, applying pressure on my G-spot. His strong hands and thick tongue had my head spinning, and all those erogenous areas stimulated at once sent a rush of trembles through my body. He stuck his fingers and tongue deeper inside both holes. I exploded all over his face.

"Damn ma, did you have to wet me up like that?" he joked, wiping my juices off of his face with his shirt.

He grabbed my leg and planted kisses from my inner thigh up to my ankle, holding my leg in the air.

"These red pumps are sexy as fuck," he whispered, kissing the top of my foot.

He removed my shoe and traced the tattoo of small *footprints that said I never walk alone* on my foot, then sucked my big toe into his mouth. I let out a guttural moan as his tongue circled around my toe. I removed my toe from his mouth and took off my other shoe. Placing both feet on his chest, I used them to massage his body all the way down to his pole. I held his hard dick in-between my feet and gently started stroking it. Loco licked his lips as he stared down at me with a lustful look.

"MMMM," he moaned. "I don't know where you get this crazy shit from ma, but it feels bomb as fuck," he stated in a low tone as his body started to shiver.

His face was distorted and his eyes were rolling back in his head; I loved his *I'm about to cum* face. I sped up the stroke with my feet. I could see his body tense and tremble. I quickly sat up and slowly sucked his rod deep into my mouth.

"FUCK!" he grunted, grabbing my head and holding it in place as he sent his seeds down my throat.

He grabbed my ankles and pulled me down toward him, and the phone started ringing. I reached for it to answer it.

"Don't touch that muthafuckin' phone," he blurted.

"It's Venus. I have to, Loco." I grabbed the phone and swiped to answer it.

"Hey girl, what's up?" I answered.

"Man, fuck that," Loco murmured, then plunged deep inside of me.

"Shit, nigga," I said when I felt the pain from his rough thrust.

"What's wrong, Kay Kay?" Venus asked.

"N-n-nothing," I stuttered, tryna play off the fact that Loco was tearing my kitty up. "You ok?"

"No girl, so much shit has happened today, and the icing on the cake is that Raquel is pregnant, so I had no choice but to completely end my relationship with Adonis once and for all. His ass hurt me for the last time," she explained.

"Umm hmm," I moan as the headboard started hitting the wall.

"Fuck, Loco," I breathed.

"Kay Kay—bitch, are you fucking?"

I didn't respond. I was lost in the pleasure that Loco's thick, long dick was giving me.

"EEEEW! You nasty, trifling ass hoe, get the fuck off my line with that shit," she chuckled before ending the call. I let the phone drop to the floor as Loco pounded deeper inside of me.

After having a massive orgasm, I laid back on my pillow, waiting for my body to recuperate. Loco went into the bathroom to relieve himself. His phone vibrated and the name Niecy flashed across the screen. I got tired of bitches throwing pussy at my nigga all the fucking time. I wasn't one of those jealous ass girlfriends; I was secure with my shit, but I promise I was about to fuck me up a bitch. I picked up his phone.

"Yes," I answered.

"Let me speak to Loco," the bitch snickered into the phone.

"Who's this?" I asked, trying to be polite just in case it wasn't one of his ex-hoes.

"Who the fuck is this?" she questioned with a ratchet ass attitude, and I was ready to jump through the phone and smack her simple ass.

"Bitch, you on my nigga line asking for him and—" This bitch burst into laughter.

"Bitch please, Loco over there selling yo ass pipe dreams, filling yo head up with bullshit; girl, he fucks every bitch that opens her legs, and you sweetie, are just his flavor of the night," she cut me off, continuing to laugh. "Bitch, he was just with me last night."

My blood was boiling and I was ready to find this hoe and beat the fuck out of her. I wasn't mad because of what she was saying. I knew she was lying; his ass was with me every night. I was pissed 'cause this thirst bucket was tryna play me like I had boo boo the fool written across my fuckin' forehead.

"You pathetic ass bird bitch, making up lies and shit; my nigga don't want you," I chuckled.

"Pathetic? You funny; you the one sharing a nigga that gives his dick away like he Oprah Winfrey," she laughed at her own stupid joke. "You so fuckin' stupid, but don't worry; when I see you bitch, I'ma fuck you up and hopefully knock some sense into yo fuckin' head," she added.

"Ok telephone gangsta, you will see me, and then we will see how much shit you talk—now get the fuck off my nigga line, thirsty ass cum bucket." I ended the call just as Loco was coming out of the bathroom.

Loco

I stepped out of the bathroom and walked into World War III. Kaylee was fuming, and I had no clue what was going on.

"I'm tired of these chicken head ass thots calling you!" she shouted as my phone went flying past my head when I stepped out of the bathroom; I side stepped right before it hit me.

"What the fuck going on, Kaylee?" I asked, trying to put on my boxer briefs.

My phone started vibrating again, but before I could answer, Kay Kay snatched it outta my hand.

"Bitch, didn't I tell you to get off my nigga line?" she asked, answering my phone.

"Who the fuck is that?" I asked, walking.

"Some bitch name Niecy," she replied, pressing speaker before she handed me the phone.

I shook my head. Niecy was a hoe I used to fuck every once in a while; she kept begging a nigga to come fuck her, and I told her over and over that I was in a relationship and didn't want her to contact me anymore. I warned this bitch.

"Bitch, why the fuck you on my muthafuckin' line? I told yo ass not to call me no more. You stupid or something?" I questioned her.

"Loco, fuck that bitch; she probably look like a ugly ass troll anyway. I'm gon' fuck her ass up. Shit, you know you gon' get tired of her real soon, and I'll be right here waiting for you, boo," she rambled on. I let her talk only because I wanted her to do exactly what she did.

"Bitch, you just signed yo death certificate; enjoy your life while you still got it," I told her.

I meant what I said; that bitch was gonna die for talking reckless to and about my girl. I played no games when it came to mine. Kay Kay was mugging me and bouncing her weight on one leg.

"Loco, I'm fuckin' that bitch up on sight, and you better tell the rest of them to stay in their fuckin' lane; get these has been ass bitches in check before I fuck you and them up," she mushed my head, then headed to the bathroom.

"Baby, I ain't touched another bitch since I touched you. Fuck them hoes, they never meant shit to me. I don't want them bitches or I would be with them. I just want you, Kay Kay." I grabbed her around her waist and pulled her to me. "You the only woman I need." I kissed her, filling her mouth with my touch.

She moaned into my mouth as I backed her up against the sink. I untied her robe as I lifted her onto the counter. She stroked my dreads as she gazed deeply into my eyes.

"I better be all the woman you need 'cause I love you." She raised her eyebrows, then planted a light kiss on my lips.

"You have to say that L word shit, don't you?" I stroked her hair and gave her another kiss.

"I have to call Venus and check on her," she said as I moved my way down her neck.

"Go ahead, I need to check on my man anyway." I picked her up off the countertop and placed her back on the floor. "We good, ma?" I asked.

She smiled and said, "Yeah, we good." I gave her a peck and headed out of the bathroom.

I went to the kitchen to get my Henny out of the freezer. I leaned against the counter, waiting for Adonis to answer his phone.

"Fuck you want nigga," he answered.

"Nigga fuck you, how the hell you doing?" I asked.

"I'm good, I guess," he replied.

"Where you at?" I asked.

"Just hittin' 46th St on my way to Lavelle's," he answered.

"Yo, so you got Venus and that bitch knocked up, fuck nigga. You ain't strap up?" I shook my head.

"Ion wanna talk about that shit, nigga. I'm fucked up right now," he said.

"I feel you, nigga; look, chill the hell out and I'll hit you later. You staying at Lavelle's tonight?" I questioned.

"Nah, I'm just gon' chill here, try to relax my mind and get my head right before going in the house and dealing with this bitch," he replied.

"Aight nigga, be easy." I ended the call.

I finished my Henny and headed upstairs to give Kay Kay some more of this grade A beef that was already on brick.

Adonis

As I approached the front gate of Lavelle's house, I noticed a man dressed in all-black standing at the door. I grabbed my gun from the small of my back and held it down at my side so that it remained unseen. The sound of the gate opening and closing got the attention of the mystery man; he turned around, and it was the same familiar guy from the funeral.

"Well, look who finally grew the fuck up," he chuckled.

I stood a couple of feet away, just in case I had to pop his ass. He moved off the steps, and that familiar feeling came back. The way he moved, his voice, I wished it wasn't so dark or he didn't have the black ass brim hat on covering his face. I squinted my eyes tryna make out his features to see who the fuck he was. He must have noticed that I didn't recognize him, 'cause he shook his head and laughed. That's when it clicked in my head; that laugh, I could recognize it anywhere.

"Eric muthafuckin' Stevens—what the fuck's up, my nigga," I beamed, giving my nigga some dap and a brotherly hug.

We walked into the house and I grabbed us a bottle of 15-year-old Crozet Cognac XO Gold and poured us both a glass. He unbuttoned his suit jacket and sat in the chair, crossing his ankle on his knee and showing off his over $21,000 Arca patent leather shoes by Corthay.

"Nigga, look at you, looking like a boss and shit; that's what happens when you become Pharaoh Conway's right-hand?" I chuckled.

"Man, that shit is wild; all them years, I followed their asses tryna get in the crew," he snickered.

"I guess Con putting that scar on your ugly ass mug wasn't enough for you ass to stay the fuck away, huh?" I asked, taking a sip.

His eyes got a little glossy and distant, like his thoughts went far away.

"Man, I miss Con's crazy ass." He shook his head and exhaled a low sigh.

"I can't believe you married Pharaoh's daughter; shit, how the fuck did that happen?" I asked.

"Shit nigga, that a movie type story," he laughed. "I can see the trailer now: kidnapping, murda, revenge, and love," he added in a fake movie trailer voice. We both started laughing. "No, seriously though; love is tricky, and my crazy ass had to fall in love with Con's granddaughter."

"Right, and they didn't end your life; shit, I got to hear the story." I shook my head in disbelief;

if I knew nothing else about the Conways, I knew they didn't fuck around when it came to family.

"Man, it's a long story but if you ask my wife, she would simply say I fell in love with a bad guy," he smiled at the thought.

"Nigga, enough about me; last I heard, you and Venus broke up. How in the fuck did you fuck that up?" he inquired.

"Man, I made a lot of mistakes, and now I think she really ain't fuckin' with a nigga. Shit, yo married ass; got any advice on this love shit?" I refilled our glasses.

"Shit nigga, I wish I did. I fucked up too many times with Ariel." He took a sip of his drink.

"Ariel? What the fuck is this, the little mermaid muthafucka? Eric and Ariel, nigga," I joked.

"Adonis and Venus; what the fuck is this, Greek mythology nigga? A god and a goddess like shit, muthafucka," he shot back.

"Well played," I laughed, lifting my glass.

"Man I tell you, Ariel had a nigga begging like a bitch. I ain't talkin' 'bout no Keith Sweat type beggin', I'm talkin' 'bout that old school James Brown please, please, please type beggin'." We burst out laughing "That nigga did a whole damn song beggin' a bitch not to make him go," he added.

The mention of that song had me reflecting back to the summers in Chicago. Eric was the bad boy in the neighborhood, being that he spent time in juvie for killing his pops, just like Loco; then, he was running the streets hustling, tryna make a come up any way he could. He was the one who taught Lavelle how to win in this game. Even though my grandmother knew everything about him, she never judged him and allowed Lavelle to hang out with him, unlike other people in the neighborhood. I was a young nigga then, so I wasn't allowed to go with them, but whenever Eric came over, he treated me like a little brother. When he told us about his childhood, I couldn't imagine killing my father but after today, I felt exactly what he must have felt.

"Ight nigga, enough with all the pleasantries and trips down memory lane; what the hell is this bullshit I'm hearing about Lavelle crossing Frank? I know my nigga and he was loyal as fuck, so I know this is a bunch of bullshit," he said.

"You and I both know Lavelle would have never crossed Frank, but man, I really don't know what the fuck going on. But I intend to find out. My brother ain't no fuckin' snake and these muthafuckas gon' pay." I was pissed all over again.

"So tell me what you know." He poured another drink, then adjusted himself in the chair.

"Man, this shit don't make sense. I mean, nothing is adding up, no matter how many times I go over it in my head. First, our traps was getting hit left and right; we still haven't found out who the fuck was responsible for that shit, then Frank's club was shot up; still no answers, then this deal with Rojas wasn't adding up and money kept coming up short. Now, my brother was killed and they blaming him for this shit" I explained.

Eric was sitting back in the chair with frowned brows, rubbing his chin and looking deep in thought. I poured myself another drink, sat back, and waited for him to speak. A few more minutes of silence went by, then he cleared his throat and spoke.

"Tell me about this deal with Rojas," he said.

"Shit, all I know is he was supplying Frank for thousands of dollars less than he normally would. I know the deal took a while because he wasn't fuckin' with Frank while he was under attack. Even though we never found the niggas responsible, shit got cleaned up quick and the deal was on, but the amount of product wasn't adding up to the amount of money being made; that's what had Frank on edge and he blamed Lavelle, even though he wasn't the one handling the deal," I told him everything that I knew.

"Who was handling the deal?" he asked.

"Frank's son Maurice; under Lavelle, of course," I replied.

"What's yo plan?" he asked.

"Simple, I want to find a way to negotiate a deal with Rojas, then take over their whole operation and dead their asses," I spoke truthfully.

"You got the manpower for that?" he questioned.

I started to feel like I was in an interrogation room, but I knew he had reasons behind all the questions.

"I got a few, but I know I need more. Taking down Frank ain't gon' be an easy job, but it's a must and I'm gon' take them down or die trying." I looked him dead in the eyes so he knew I was serious about my shit. "I already got my nigga Beans looking into Maurice and his deal with Rojas," I continued.

"Well look, here's what I can do. I can lead you to the Red Sea, but I can't get you to the promise land; in other words, I can get you the info on the deal with Rojas, and set up a meet with you and him to air everything out. I got connections to make that happen; then, I can send two of my heavy hittas to help you get them niggas, and I can supply you with some heavy ammunition. How you gon' get the money to get shit rolling? You got some stacked?"

"I do, plus Lavelle has a stash spot and he just got a shipment of merch that I put away, so I'm gon' move that shit then I'll be straight. I got that, Eric, trust me; just get me the info and the extra shit, and I'm gon' handle this shit. I will get my revenge." I had to let him know I wasn't that same lil' nigga that was pressed to run behind him and Lavelle. I wasn't scared to go to war with anybody, especially Frank.

"Aight, I got a flight to catch in the morning so I'm gonna head out. Give me a few days and I will get back with you on this. Go home get your head together and be ready for whatever you have to do, but make sure your head is in the game first, understand?" I nodded yes. He stood up gave me dap and a brotherly hug. "Be easy."

I decided to head home myself so I walked out, locking up Lavelle's house behind me. I walked Eric to his car, gave him another brotherly hug, then hopped into my truck.

Driving down Kenilworth Avenue heading home. I was listening to *Back From The FEDS*, Milly Montana was the truth with this mix tape. I felt better talking to Eric about the bullshit surrounding Lavelle's death. As soon as I hit 295 heading toward Richmond, my song came on and I blasted the volume and got real hyped, bobbing my head, rappin', making hand movements, and feeling the fuck outta that song

I just want the money, I just want the fuckin' money

Keep it one hundred lil bitch youon wanna fuck me you wanna fuck this money

Keep it one hundred my nigga would you still fuck with me if

The music was interrupted by my phone ringing through the speakers.

"SHIT!" I shouted.

It was Beans. I pushed the button to answer.

"What yo old ass doing up this late, nigga? It's almost 9 o'clock, ain't it past yo bed time, muthafucka?" I chuckled.

"Naw nigga, I just finished fuckin' this p.y.t, you know what I mean," he responded proudly.

"Nigga, ain't nobody lettin' you stick yo shriveled up wrinkled ass dick in their pussy; go somewhere with that bullshit. What the fuck you calling me for?" I asked, getting down to business.

"Where you at?" he asked in a serious tone.

"Just hit 295, what's up?" I answered.

"Meet me at my studio. I got info for you," he stated.

"On my way." I hung up and took the next exit and headed back to Kenilworth Avenue.

I knocked on the steel door to Beans' studio. I heard the camera move so that he could see who was knocking. I gave him the finger in the camera. He buzzed me in.

"Nigga, what the fuck you think this is, Fort Knox and shit?" I snickered as I walked over to him.

"Why the hell you got to give me a hard time, Adonis?" he asked, knowing damn well he loved it.

"Cause, Beans, I love fuckin' with yo old ass," I laughed.

"So did your brother," he said with a hint of sadness. "Adonis, I'm sorry about what happened to Lavelle and I know you had a fucked up day, but I'm about to make it just a little better."

He handed me an envelope, and I opened it. It was pictures of Maurice and a couple of young niggas that I didn't recognize.

"Beans, who these niggas with Maurice?" I quizzed.

"Apparently, Maurice is setting up shop in Detroit," he replied.

"Detroit, what the fuck Frank doing setting up in shop Michigan?" I was confused.

"This has nothing to do with Frank, Adonis; this is all Maurice, and I can put money on the fact that these was the niggas hitting the traps," he informed me.

"Yeah, I agree. That would explain why nobody knew shit about these niggas. Damn, I know this nigga is dirty, doing side deals on his pops. What the fuck he planning?" I was really confused; I needed to find shit out quick.

"You find out about Rojas yet?" I asked.

"Naw, but I can stay on it," he said.

"Nah, I got that, just keep eyes on Maurice 'til we figure shit out." I reached into my pocket and pulled out a stack. "Here is 10 grand; I'll get the rest to you when we finish this shit."

"Nigga, you just carry this type of money on you?" he asked with furrowed brows.

"No nigga, I just had it today. Stay the fuck outta my pockets anyway, old man," I chuckled, then left.

I was mentally, emotionally, and physically exhausted by the time I got home. I was hoping Raquel was already sleep 'cause I was not in the mood to hear her fuckin' mouth. The strong smell of bleach hit me as soon as I reached the top of the stairs.

"What the fuck was she cleaning?" I asked myself.

I opened the bedroom door and she was sitting on the bed texting. Without even acknowledging her, I went straight to my closet and took off my clothes, then I proceeded to go into the bathroom to take a shower. I opened the door, and the bleach smell was so strong I started to cough.

"What the fuck!" I shouted, noticing a pile of shoes and clothes in the tub with bleach poured all over them.

I looked at Raquel, and she was sitting on the bed smirking with her arms folded. I was furious and if she wasn't pregnant, I would have jumped on that bed and beat the shit outta her. I covered my nose with the arm of my shirt and walked over to the tub to see what she bleached. This bitch bleached all my expensive shit; Gucci, Givenchy, Ferragamo, just to name a few—shit I wore on a daily basis. Yes, it was material and replaceable, but that was beside the point. This was shit that I spent my muthafuckin' money on. I picked up the toilet brush and started sorting through the clothes to see exactly what she bleached, and I came across my authentic, autographed Doug Williams Redskins jersey. The anger grew inside of me so fast that I had to have a real woosah moment 'cause I was about to strangle that bitch. First, I had that jersey for a long ass time. Lavelle took me to a Redskins' event and bought that jersey. Doug Williams was there, and he signed it for me; that shit is irreplaceable. I swear I could kill that bitch.

After taking a moment to calm down, I decided to go into the other room to take a shower and sleep. When I came out of the bathroom, Raquel was sitting on the edge of the bed, legs and arms crossed, bouncing with an *I don't give a fuck* look on her face. I went to the dresser and got some boxer briefs, shorts, and a t-shirt. I was strolling around the room like she wasn't even there. I could see the anger written all over her face, but I refused to give her the reaction that she wanted.

Raquel

I couldn't believe that this nigga was walking around the room as if he didn't see me sitting there pissed the fuck off. I thought after he saw his clothes all bleached up, we was gonna have it out, but he said nothing, not even after seeing that I bleached his precious Doug Williams jersey. I waited while he gathered his things and started out of the bedroom before uttering a word.

"Umm, excuse me, you don't see me sitting here?" I asked.

He turned around and gave me a threatening look, but I didn't give a fuck. I was pregnant, so I knew he wouldn't touch me.

"Adonis, you hear me fuckin' talking to you?" I stood up and walked toward him.

"What, you mad? You don't like the fact that I bleached your shit, nigga?" I taunted as I got up in his face; he took a deep breath and stepped back.

"So, you just gonna stand there looking at me like you wanna do something to me?" I snickered. "Awwww, what's wrong, cat got your tongue?" I teased. "Are you upset 'cause you couldn't stay with yo bitch? She don't want you no more? Why, 'cause I got yo baby in my stomach?" I exasperated.

"Raquel, I'm warning you—leave me the fuck alone," he said through clenched teeth as his jaws tightened and his nose flared. He stormed out of the room, and I followed behind him still ranting.

"I'm not gonna let you carry me for that bitch; she left you, and now her trifling disrespectful ass—" My words were cut short.

Adonis grabbed me by the throat, slamming me against the wall so hard that I lost my breath. He pinned his body against mine as he squeezed my neck tighter. I clawed and kicked at him, trying to free myself from his grip, but Adonis squeezed tighter. His eyes were filled with rage; pure evil, like he intended on killing me. I could feel the fear rising inside as my eyes felt like they were gonna pop out of my head.

"You are only here because you carrying my baby; what part of that don't you understand? I don't love you, I don't need you, and I sho as hell don't want you. If I fuck Venus or any other bitch out here, it ain't yo business; we ain't together, now get that through your thick skull." He banged my head against the wall. "If you ever try that shit again or speak of Venus with such disrespect, baby or not, I will kill you with my bare hands. Now get yo ass in there and clean that shit up." His voice was penetrating through my soul as spit flew out of his mouth with a tense look on his face.

He let me go, pushing me to the side. I slid down the wall tryna catch my breath. Although he wasn't choking me for long, it felt like an eternity and I knew my life was over. I never seen such hate in his eyes, nor had he spoken to me with so much venom in his voice. I placed my hand around my neck and rubbed it as I shed tears. Adonis went about his business like he really didn't give a fuck. I got up off the ground, hurried to the room, and grabbed my cell phone. I went downstairs to get trash bags so that I could clean up the mess that I made. I got to the kitchen and peeked around the corner, making sure I didn't hear Adonis coming. I quickly scrolled down my contact list to the person I was looking for.

"What's up?" he answered.

"Change of plans. I know you just wanted Adonis out of the way so you can do what you got to do."

"Yeah, what do we need to do differently?"

"Instead of leaving him alive, I want the bitch ass nigga dead; he wanna treat me like shit after I had to fake being nice to his stupid ass, and he threatened our baby. Kill him, and make it a slow death."

"Gladly, that muthafucka will pay."

I hung up and went to clean up the mess.

Venus

The ringing phone awakened me, so I picked it up and saw that it was Adonis.

"Adonis, what do you want?" I answered, irritated 'cause he woke me up.

"You, for real for real, but since I can't have you yet, I just wanna know how Moms doing?" he asked.

"She's fine, Adonis; she's sleeping just like I was," I snapped.

"And Harmony?" he giggled a little.

"She sleep too, Adonis; now what do you want, I want to go back to bed," I whined.

"I want you to give me another chance; let me show you that I can be the man that you need," he stated. I exhaled a frustrated sigh before speaking.

"Adonis, I meant what I said; you hurt me for the last time. Now go be happy with yo hoe. Where is she anyway while you on my line talkin' nonsense?" I questioned.

"Man, fuck that bitch. I told you I'm not with her; she in one room and I'm in the other. The stupid as slut bleached my shit." I laughed lightly. "Venus, that shit ain't funny; don't make me come all the way over there and give yo ass a good spanking," he said, obviously flirting.

"Adonis, spank yo dick; good night." I hung up the phone.

He called back, but I didn't answer. I laid my head back down on the pillow and my phone chimed. It was a text from Adonis.

Him: *"You wrong for that but it's cool tho I'm still not giving up on us tho*

Me: GN *Adonis*

Him*: GN*

I smiled. I didn't know if I could actually completely let him go. I loved him too much, and he knew me too damn well. Maybe his mother was right; Adonis was my man, fuck that hoe. Who cared if she had a baby? It wasn't like I couldn't handle the bitch if I needed to. Shit, if I wasn't pregnant, I woulda fuck her ass up in that fuckin' limo. Shit, I knew the bitch was gon' keep taking shots at me on the low, so I was sure I would get my opportunity once we had these babies. I really didn't give a shit about being cordial for the kids—fuck her. Harmony and this baby were gonna have a relationship with Adonis no matter what. Adonis would murk that bitch if she tried to keep him away from his baby.

Laying in the dark tryna get back to sleep, I started thinking about Adonis talking about giving me a good spanking. I got horny as hell, and it took everything in me not to call his ass and tell him to come on. Just as I was thinking about him, he was thinking about me 'cause he sent me a text.

Him: *I really wanna come and smack that ass*

Me: *I really want you to*

Him: *Don't play It ain't shit for me to be on my way*

I thought about it for a moment, not sure if I was making the right choice, but fuck it; like his mother said, that was my man, and I would fuck him whenever I chose.

Me: *Come on*

30 minutes later, I was in the living room pacing the floor, wondering if I was making a mistake by telling him to come over. I didn't want him to think that sex meant we were gonna get back together, or that he could come in and outta of my life as he pleased. I heard the front door open and close. My heart started racing. Adonis walked into the living room looking like he just rolled outta bed.

"So you waiting on daddy, huh?" He had a cocky smirk on his face, and I wanted to knock it right off.

"You know what, Adonis? This is a mistake. I'm sorry," I apologized.

I shouldn't have made him drive over here knowing in my heart that I was making a mistake.

"Venus, don't give me that shit; you can fight this all you want, but we love each other and it's nothing we can do about it," he said.

"Adonis, you just got outta bed with another woman; how can you think this shit is right for either of us?" I asked.

He walked over to me and said, "I was in the other room, not in bed with her, and this is right because we belong together. I don't care about Raquel being pregnant, you do." He moved the curls that fell in my face and lifted my chin up. "I love you, Venus; that's the truth." He kissed me.

As his tongue filled my mouth, I knew in my heart what he was saying was true. We belonged together. He grabbed my hand and walked me to the basement like we did when we were younger so his mother couldn't hear us sneaking to have sex. Once in the basement, Adonis took me in his arms and kissed me; our mouths felt like one and his tongue flickered against mine. His hands ran through my soft curls as my hands caressed his deep waves in his hair. Without breaking our kiss, he walked me into the basement bedroom. He slowly slid down the spaghetti strap on my tank top, kissing me on my shoulder; the passion he held in his eyes burned deep within my soul. He slowly pulled my shirt over my head, then planted soft kisses from my stomach to the middle of my chest; making his way to my neck, he sucked, licked, and lightly bit my skin, causing quivers down my spine. He grabbed the back of my neck and waist, then pulled me into a deep, sensual kiss. As his tongue darted in and out of my mouth, he traced my lips with his tongue as his warm minty breath mixed with mine. He laid me on the bed, then slowly removed my bottoms. He kissed, then licked my belly button as he slid his fingers up and down my clit. He licked me from my belly button to my hard nipples and kissed them as if he was tongue kissing my mouth.

"MMMMM!" I let out a deep, guttural moan as I squirmed underneath him.

He raised up enough to remove his clothes. I reached up and started stroking his dick. Staring deep into my eyes, he grabbed me by the back of my head, pulled me up, and guided his soft dick into my mouth. I stroked the shaft, grinding it like a pepper mill as I sucked and licked him, making love to his pole with my mouth. Our eyes were glued on each other as I twirled my tongue around the head, flicking it in and out of the hole.

"Shit!" he hissed, rubbing his hands through my hair.

I made sure his rod was nice and wet. I continued stroking it as I sucked on his balls. Adonis grew so big and hard in my mouth; it felt like I was sucking on a billy club. He grabbed me by the back of my neck and laid me down. He climbed on top of me, kissing me slowly as he used his knee to spread my legs. He entered me slowly as he laid completely on top of me and wrapped my legs around his waist. I rolled my hips slowly to match the rhythm of his slow grind. Kissing me, caressing my body, and nibbling on my collar bone, Adonis made love to me; it was slow, sensual, and passionate with skin to skin contact the entire time. Staring deeply into my eyes, he whispered *I love you* before we both climaxed.

"Where do we go from here? Just tell me and I will do whatever I have to do," Adonis asked.

I laid my head on his chest. "I don't know, but we can't keep doing this; it's not good for either one of us." I kissed his chest.

"Venus, just say the word and it's done," he said.

"Right now, Adonis, let's not talk. Ok?"

He nodded his head and pulled me tighter. We laid in silence, holding each other until sleep found us.

Kay Kay

"FUCK!" I shouted, shaking my steering wheel. I turned the key in the ignition for the fifth time, and still nothing. I let out a loud, frustrated sigh as I dug my phone out of my purse. I scrolled down to *My Nigga* and hit talk. The phone started ringing.

"Come on, nigga; answer the fuckin' phone," I mumbled to myself as the phone continued ringing in my ear.

"You have reached That Nigga, please leave a message after the tone...beep!"

His voice mail came on. Instead of leaving a message, I decided to shoot him a quick text.

Me: *My car won't start can you come get me*

I waited for his response. A few minutes later, my phone pinged.

My Nigga: *Naw I'm busy right now catch a Uber to the shop on St. Barnabas Rd. I will meet you there.*

"What the fuck?" I said "This nigga got me fucked up. I'm not catching a fuckin' Uber to the shop, what the fuck for?" I ranted to myself.

I scrolled to *My Ace* and hit talk.

"Hey girl," Venus answered, sounding cheerful.

"Hey, what you doing?" I asked.

"What's wrong?" she questioned, noticing the frustration in my voice.

"My car won't start and I'm stuck Bowie Maryland. Loco is busy somewhere and can't come; can you come get me?" I asked.

"Shit Kaylee, I'm with Adonis and Harmony at Potomac Mills," she replied.

"Fuck, you all the way in Virginia, and what the hell? I thought you was done with him." I couldn't believe I was stranded and no one could come and get me.

"Girl I am, but we will talk later; catch an Uber and call Triple A," she said.

She only added to my frustration. I ended the call and called and Uber. I shot Loco a text telling him that I was waiting on the Uber, and I would text him when I was on the way.

Six minutes later, the Uber pulled up. I got out of my car and into the Uber.

"Hi, how you doing?" I spoke as I slid into the back seat.

"I'm good, and how are you?" he replied.

"I'm good," I spoke dryly as I was focused on texting Loco

Me*: I'm in the Uber on my way and you better be there when I get there*

My Nigga*: dead that fuckin' attitude I'm already here waiting on you*

"How the fuck he know I got an attitude?" I whispered to myself.

Ping! The sound of my phone alerted me of another text

My Nigga: *because I know you*

I was confused.

Me: *huh?????*

My Nigga: you was wondering how I know you got a attitude

I looked at my phone with a scrunched face; *shit, this nigga not only crazy as fuck but he psychic too.*

I arrived at the address that Loco sent me looking around confused.

"Why am I meeting him at a car dealership. I called him and he didn't answer. I texted him, but he didn't respond."

"What the fuck is going on?" I asked as I headed into the building.

He said he was already there, but I couldn't find him anywhere. I walked up to the man at the counter.

"Excuse me, I'm trying to make sure I have the right address; did a tall dark-skinned man with dreads come in here, by chance?" I asked, trying to sound pleasant and polite.

"Yeah, Loco was here; he went to the carryout at the corner," He chuckled "You must be Kay Kay," he said, extending his hand for a shake.

I nodded my head, smiling as I shook his hand.

"You can wait in here if you want," he told me.

"That's ok. I will go to the store and find him, I'm thirsty anyway," I smiled, then waved as I headed out to of the door.

I was walking down the street to the store on the corner and I spotted Loco looking like he was in a heated argument with some light-skinned ratchet-looking hood rat bitch with blond and black braids down to her back, reminding me of Ice Cube's girlfriend in the movie *Friday*. I kicked off my Jimmy Choos and ran down the street to see what the fuck was going on.

"Bitch, I gave yo ass a pass, don't make me take that shit back," I heard Loco say to the bitch as I approached.

"Loco, who the hell is this?" I asked, pointing dead at the bitch.

"Oh, that's Niecy," he answered as he took a step back.

"Oh, the telephone gangsta with all that mouth," I smirked as I adjusted my shoe in my hand.

"Who the fuck are you?"

I introduced myself to the bitch with my shoe. I hit the bitch slam in the mouth with my Jimmy Choo, then tossed them to Loco.

"Bitch, didn't I tell you that you was gon' see me? Didn't I say I was gon' fuck you up on sight?" I was raining blows down on this bitch as I questioned her, not really wanting an answer. I grabbed the bitch up by her hair and slung her into the wall. Her head bounced off the wall and she stumbled.

"You had all that fuckin' mouth on the phone, but ain't got shit to say now," I continued beating the shit out of her ass.

She tried swinging on me and landed quite a few punches, but that shit didn't matter. I had her ass against the wall by her throat.

"Stay the fuck away from my man or I will fuck you up every chance I get." I punched the bitch so hard that she fell to her knees. She was holding me by my shirt and tryna pull herself up, so I kneed her off of me and slept her ass. I stepped over her body as the crowd of onlookers burst out laughing.

"Damn, that bitch sleep like shit," I heard one guy laugh.

Loco took the napkins outta of his bag and poured some water on my feet, then wiped my Jimmy Choos clean and slid them back on. We walked back up to the car dealership eating his potato wedges with ketchup and mumbo sauce.

"What the hell took yo ass so long?" the man behind the counter asked as we walked in the door.

"My girl had something to handle, nigga; shit, yo food still warm," Loco told him with a mouthful of wedges.

"Where's the bathroom?" I asked. I wanted to make sure I was still straight.

"I'll take you," Loco said, placing his food on the counter.

We walked hand in hand down the long hallway. Loco stopped and opened the bathroom door for me. I walked in and went straight to the mirror checking my face. Loco came in and locked the door behind him.

"What are you doing?" I asked, turning around and facing him.

He walked up on me and placed his arms around my waist, and backed me against the sink.

"Man, watching you beat that bitch ass had a nigga on brick. I wanna get off in yo guts right now." He gave me a quick kiss.

"Really, Orlando Tyrell, you wanna fuck in a bathroom at a car dealership? I ain't no cheap slut, and why are we here anyway?" I asked, pushing him away from me.

I turned around and started fixing my hair; he pushed me against the sink.

"You on a need to know basis; you'll find out why we here when you need to; as far as being in the bathroom, I fuck anytime, anywhere, any place, so get used to it, and you better be the best damn slut I fuck." He unfastened my jeans and yanked them down.

Bending me over the sink, he pulled his dick out, lifted my leg up and out of my jeans, put my foot up on the sink, and thrust deep inside of me. He entered me so hard that my body jerked forward, pinning me against the mirror. Long dick muthafuckas had a way of putting you in awkward ass positions and still hitting every wall inside your kitty.

"Loco, damn this shit hurts," I groaned, tryna push him back.

"You can handle it; now shut the fuck up and let me get this nut." He pinned his body against mine while holding my waist.

I could feel his dick go deeper as it stretched my walls. He was grunting with each stroke, giving it to me hard and fast. I grabbed the edge of the sink and folded my lips in my mouth, trying not to scream; not a painful scream, but a loud pleasure-filled scream. This nigga had my pussy talking like shit; the gushing sound of my wetness every time he slammed into me echoed off the walls of the bathroom. Loco put my other leg up on the sink, spreading me wider so that he could go deeper.

"Fuck, Loco, you tryna knock my uterus out, shit," I grunted, tryna take the painful pleasure.

He sped up the pace and my pussy started making farting noises. That shit was loud as fuck bouncing off the walls. That sound only added to his excitement; he grabbed my waist and started sliding me slowly up and down his pole, staring into my eyes through the mirror.

"I love you, Loco," I moaned.

He thrust hard and deep one last time, and we both came. He laid his head on my back while slowly removing himself from inside of me.

"I love you too, Kaylee Denise," he whispered in my ear and I ain't gon' lie, I came again.

That was the first time he said those words to me, and to top that moment off, he called me by my government and I loved when he called me that. After cleaning ourselves off with rough ass paper towels, we headed back to the front.

"Bout time, nigga," the man behind the counter said as we approached him

"Fuck you, Chris; man, is my shit ready yet nigga?" Loco asked, grabbing his food.

He handed Loco some keys and said, "She's right out front waiting on you."

He led us into the parking lot and stopped in front of a red Lexus ES 350 sedan with 20-inch chrome rims to match the chrome accents on the car, and 20% VLT tinted windows. Loco looked at me with a big grin on his face and handed me the keys.

"Surprise," he beamed.

My mouth dropped.

Loco

The look on Kay Kay's face when I gave her the keys to the car was priceless. She was cheesin' like a muthafucka. She jumped on me screaming and kissing me all over my face.

"Man, stop that shit girl," I said, pushing her off of me.

"I can't believe you did this for me!" she boasted as she ran over to the driver's side and hopped into the car.

"You said you need a new car; it just so happened your car wouldn't start today," I chuckled, pulling her battery cable out of my pocket.

"So that's why my car wouldn't start?" she asked, fake poutin' like she was mad.

"You wouldn't let me do this as long as you thought your car was good, so I had to pull a trick out my sleeve," I winked and gave her a quick kiss.

"What you doing for the rest of the day?" she asked, pulling me closer into the car through the window. "I can't wait to get you home tonight, I got to thank you properly," she whispered in my ear. My jimmy instantly got hard.

"Keep talkin' like that and I'm gonna take you in the back of the parking lot and fuck you silly in the backseat of yo new whip," I warned her.

"Boy, you know I'm Beyoncé," she smirked, raising her brows up and down.

I looked at her puzzled. I had no clue what she was talking about, then she started bouncing up and down singing.

"I always keep the top tier, 5-star backseat lovin' in the car, like make that wood make that wood, holly like a boulevard."

I cracked up. "Yo silly ass," I chuckled.

Chris leaned into the passenger side of the window and started explaining all of the features to her. I halfway listened; I already knew everything about the car. My phone vibrated in my pocket. I took it out and saw that it was Adonis.

"What up, my nigga?" I answered.

"Shit nigga, where you at?" he asked.

"I'm up here with Chris and Kay Kay. I just copped her that Lexus 350 joint," I replied.

"Oh shit, you know her ass gon' be stuntin' like shit in that whip with her big ass shades on," he laughed.

I had to laugh too 'cause she was sitting in the car listening to Chris with some big ass Gucci shades on right now. I snapped a picture and sent it to Adonis. He laughed his ass off.

"I told you, nigga; her vain ass swear she fly," he started laughing again.

"Man, leave my girl alone; she is fly, with her fine ass," I snickered.

"Aight nigga, I need you to meet me at Lavelle's strip club. I need to meet with the staff to let them know what I intend on doing with the place, then we have business to discuss," he informed me. I agreed to meet him, then ended the call.

I leaned into Kay Kay's car. "Look, I have some shit I need to do so I'm 'bout to head to my house and take a quick shower. What you 'bout to do?" I asked.

"I'm headed home to take a hot bath; are you gonna be able to be at my house for dinner?" she inquired.

"I don't know, but I will definitely be there for dessert." I licked my lips before kissing her goodbye.

I watched as she put her shades on and drove off.

"She's beautiful," Chris complimented, patting me on the shoulder. "I can't believe yo ass is on lock down now." He shook his head.

"Yeah man, she got me," I admitted.

"Yeah, got yo ass buyin' cars and fuckin' in my bathroom and shit," he pointed out.

I laughed. "Man, I can't keep my hands off her," he laughed. "Nigga, good lookin' out on the car, thanks." I gave him dap.

"Anytime, you know I got you."

We chopped it up for a few minutes and I headed home to take a quick shower and go meet Adonis.

Adonis

Thinking about the way Eric sat in my chair dressed and carrying himself like a boss had me thinking about making changes myself. Everything Lavelle did screamed boss, and now that everything he owned was mine, I had to think like a boss. I had new ideas to step up our game. I stepped into my closet and pulled out my dark charcoal gray Giorgio Armani suit, and paired it with my black Gucci loafers. I got dressed and checked myself out in the mirror. Satisfied with the way I looked, I grabbed my keys and headed out the door.

I pulled in the parking lot of Escapades just as my phone began ringing.

"What's up, brah?" I answered. It was Eric.

"What's up? What you up to?" he asked.

"I'm taking pointers from you. I got my head in the game, and now I'm about to go in here and let these employees know what I intend to do with the business," I told him.

"Good, handle yo shit like a boss at all times," he advised.

"Got you, so what's up?" I was hoping he was calling with some information so I could put my plan into action.

"I got what you need; there was never a deal on the table with Rojas," he stated, and I was floored.

"What the fuck? What you mean it was never a deal on the table? Who in the hell they were doing business with? How in the hell did this shit go over Lavelle's head?" I was firing off questions fast as shit. I couldn't believe what Eric just told me.

"Only question I can answer is Rojas met with Maurice one time and refused to do business with him, so the who, what, where, and whys, I have no clue about. I could look into it deeper if you want, but I convinced Rojas to meet with you and discuss this situation as well as do business with you; only thing is, he's in California for a few weeks longer, so you got to be ready to move when he's ready. I'm not available to go with you for about two weeks, so I can try to set the meeting up then if that's good for you," he said.

My mind was racing tryna figure all this shit out; I guess meeting with Rojas would be the best way to get some of the answers that I needed.

"Aight, make the necessary arrangements and let me know, and I'll be there." He agreed and we got off the phone. I got out the car and headed into the building.

"What's up, boss man?" Tito said, giving me dap.

"Everybody here?" I asked.

"Yep," he answered.

"Aight, lock the door and send them all into the meeting room," I spoke with authority.

I went into the meeting room and took my rightful place at the head of the table. I felt like I belonged there; I was the boss now. Lavelle set the bar high, and I had some big shoes to fill. Everyone came into the room and took a seat around the table. I sat up proudly as I began to speak.

"First, I would like to thank everyone for hanging in there with me. I had to get my head back in the game, and thanks for holding shit down in my absence." I waited as Loco passed out folders containing my changes to everyone, then I introduced him as a manager.

"This will no longer be a strip club; it will now be a nightclub. I want it to be just as classy as this club is. Ladies, you will no longer dance; however, you will be bottle girls, and servers. If you feel that is something you don't want to do, feel free to empty your lockers and leave. Tito, you will remain head of security, and I need you to pick some guards for the new VIP lounge; other than that, the rest of the security team will carry out their jobs as normal. Bartenders, you will continue your jobs as well. Kid West, since we will no longer have dancers, you won't need to emcee. Just spin music, and I want to try to have performers come. On those days, if they use you that's fine; but if they don't, you can chill until it's time for you to take over the music. Management will remain the same, with the addition of Loco. He is directly under me; if I'm not available then go to him. Also, we will be closed for renovations until further notice, but everyone will still get paid as normal except the dancers; you will get paid the amount quoted in the packet for bottle girls, minus the tips. Lastly, the name will be changed to Virgo Lounge; as we all know, Lavelle is a Virgo, so let's honor him by making this the best damn club in D.C." I looked around the room at all the faces to make sure everyone understood the changes.

"Anyone have a problem with what's being changed or simply don't want to be a part of the team anymore, feel free to get up and walk away now." I waited for anyone to leave. Destiny raised her hand.

"Speak, Destiny," I commanded.

"How are we gonna make the amount of money being bottle girls that we did dancing?" she questioned.

"Well, you have a set amount that is fair; however, just like you got on that stage poppin' yo pussy and shakin' yo ass for a nigga to make it rain, step up yo customer service game and treat these niggas like you want their money and I promise, they will still fill yo pockets. The difference is you make them niggas respect you while they giving you their money," I said.

"I think I like that," she said with a smile on her face.

"Anyone have any more questions?" I asked, looking around the room.

After no one had any questions, I dismissed them until further notice. Loco, Smoke, and I headed to the office so we could discuss the other business. We got into the office and I grabbed the Henny out of the mini bar fridge and poured us all a glass.

"Man, you sounded almost like Lavelle in there," Smoke said with a half-smile.

"'Preciate that, man." I took a sip of the Henny and sat down in the chair behind the desk. "Ok, two things; on the way here, I got a call from Eric and he informed me that there was never a deal between Maurice and Rojas," I informed them.

"Wait, so that nigga was lying about that shit the whole time?" Smoke asked with bass in his voice; he was pissed.

"I'm saying that snake set my brother up for failure, and I'm gonna get to the bottom of all of this shit. I got a meeting with Rojas for some time within the next two weeks, and I want y'all to come with me."

Loco didn't say a word, but the look on his face let me know that he was ready to kill.

"Beans also informed me that Maurice is setting something up in Detroit. I'm gonna find out what it is and put an end to it. We gonna take over whatever operation he got going on. I want to make them niggas come after me but first, we going to California to meet with Rojas; when we get back, we gonna hit Frank's biggest traps. I want to take everything and kill whoever inside. I want him to know that I'm coming for him. I want everything they have. You feel me?"

"Hell yeah nigga, now you speaking my language," Loco boasted. Smoke agreed.

I told them that I would call them with the details as soon as Eric called me. We left out of the office. Smoke went around making sure no one was in the building and everything was secured as Loco and I waited.

"So you goin' to Kay Kay's now?" I asked.

"Yeah, I have to make I quick stop, I have something to take care of," he stressed in a toneless voice.

I didn't want to know what the hell the nigga had planned, and knowing him like I do, it was probably best that I didn't know. Loco was smart, so I wasn't worried that whatever he had to do would interfere in my business. I took my phone out of my pocket and sent Venus a text.

Me: *Can I come over*

Her: *No Adonis*

Me: *Aight it's cool selfish ass*

Her: *smh bye boy*

Me: *I ain't no boy when I be layin' down the pipe*

Her*: Nasty ass*

I laughed and put the phone back in my pocket just as Smoke came out of the back. I turned off the lights and locked the door of Escapades for the last time.

When I reached the top of the steps, I heard Raquel tell somebody I was home and she had to go. She was talking slightly above a whisper.

"You don't have to get off the phone 'cause I came in; you can talk to whatever nigga you want, I don't give a fuck." I took my jacket off and hung it up.

"Adonis, please; why would I be talking to another nigga when I'm having your baby?" she shook her head and looked at me with a scrunch face.

"All I'm saying is I don't give a fuck," I reiterated as I gathered my things and headed to the other room to take a shower.

Loco

I headed home to gather a few things that I needed to carry out my plan. I parked my car in the driveway, then went into the house and changed clothes. I grabbed some trash bags, a bottle of Henny, a bottle of Oleander out of the safe under the cabinet in the garage, and some weed. I took the covering off my lil' black hooptie, changed the tags, then headed out.

I parked a few buildings down from Niecy's house, then crept around the back and made my way to her house. I walked up to her door, then took the Dr. Scholl's insoles that I glued together and attached them to the bottom of my shoes. I slipped on my gloves and pressed the button for her doorbell, then took the gloves off.

"Who is it?" she called out.

I didn't respond knowing that the dumb bitch was already looking out of the peephole.

"What you want?" she asked. I held up the bottle of Hennessey and the bag of weed.

"I'm sorry," I lied, knowing the pressed bitch would fall for it.

She opened the door and stepped to the side, allowing me to come in.

"I told yo bitch you would be back," she smirked as we walked into the living room.

"Man, fuck her; we through. She think I'm still fuckin' with you so I said fuck it, I might as well, and now I'm here to apologize," I lied.

"Here, roll this up while I go fix us a drink," I instructed as I passed her the blunt that I already gutted and had in the bag with the oleander, then passed her bag of weed.

I went into the kitchen, put my gloves back on, then grabbed two glasses out of the cabinet. I pulled out the oleander and crushed it into her glass, then filled it with the Hennessy. I poured myself a glass, then joined her in the living room. She was licking the blunt to seal it when I sat on the coffee table and passed her the drink.

"Before you spark that, let's make a toast," I insisted.

By licking the blunt, she already had poison in her system; plus, I didn't want to breathe that toxic shit in. She agreed to a toast.

"To the beginning of something real," I flashed her a sexy look as I smiled.

She had a big goofy ass grin on her face. She lifted the glass and took a sip.

"No baby, we gotta take this down like shots," I chuckled as I gulped mine down and poured another.

She gulped hers down and I poured her another glass; she was unaware that I put the twigs from the oleander in the bottle after I poured my second drink. She gulped that one down, then placed the blunt in her mouth but before she could grab the lighter, the oleander started to take effect. She started sweating profusely.

"Damn, why in the hell am I sweating like this?" She used her shirt to wipe the sweat away.

"You ok?" I asked, faking concern.

She started gagging as if she was about to vomit. I grabbed a trash bag and held it up to her as she violently vomited into it. She started coughing and gasping for air. I knew it wouldn't be long before she fell unconscious.

"I warned you, didn't I? I told you to stop calling me and talking shit to my girl; now you got to pay with yo life." She tried reaching for me as she struggled to breathe. I stepped out of her way.

Heaving and clenching her chest, she tried to reach for her phone, but I snatched it up.

"You got to be quicker than that," I snickered, mimicking the State Farm commercial.

She tried to get up, but I tripped her, sending her crashing down onto the floor in front on the couch. A look of terror came across her face.

"I told you that you signed your death certificate," I reminded her of the last thing I said to her on the phone that night.

I sat back down on the coffee table and watched her slip into a state of unconsciousness, then I placed my gloves on and pulled out two bags of pure cocaine and mixed it into the Henny and poured it in her mouth. Everybody knew Niecey liked to party a lot and most of the time, she was poppin' molly or e-pills, Xanax, or any other pill they sold. She also liked push that white in her nose or lace it in her weed, so it wouldn't surprise nobody if she overdosed. Holding her mouth closed so the drink couldn't spill out, I tossed her head back and made it go down her throat. I put the remainder of Henny, the empty bag of weed, and the blunt into the trash bag. I put some of her vomit in her mouth and on the floor beside her, then placed the bag in it with the rest of the stuff. I put the two bags of cocaine on her table, rubbed some of the residue on my finger, and stuck it in her nose. I took off the gloves, replacing them with a fresh pair. I sat on her coffee table going through her phone, deleting all our texts and my contact information from her phone, then I replaced her memory card and battery with a new one, threw it under the couch, and sat and waited with a mirror to make sure she stopped breathing. I checked her pulse in multiple places and when I discovered that she didn't have one, I gave her place a once over, making sure I covered all my tracks. I stood over her dead body.

"Rest in peace, bitch." I kissed my cross, then left out the back door.

I made my way to my car and got the hell outta there. I pulled off of the highway and went behind an abandoned building, took the trash bag out of the front seat, and smashed it until it was nothing tiny shards of glass, then dumped the contents into the dumpster. I ripped the trash bags into pieces and tossed it in there as well, then I went home, changed the tags on my hooptie, and covered it back up. I went into the house, took a shower, got in my truck, and headed to Kay Kay's house to get my dessert.

Two weeks later

Adonis

We arrived at LAX airport, and Eric was waiting at the terminal with two guys.

"What the fuck is up?" he asked, giving me a brotherly hug.

"These are my niggas, Loco and Smoke; this is my nigga Eric," I introduced them to Eric.

"Loco, I have a nigga on my team named Loco, and he's a crazy muthafucka; what about you?" he asked, shaking his hand.

"See, I tell people I ain't crazy, I'm fuckin' psycho," he replied.

Eric nodded his head with raised brows. "I think I like this nigga already," he chuckled, then introduced us to Tony and Sam, the two niggas he had with him.

After collecting our luggage, we headed to The Hollywood Hotel near Santa Monica where

Rojas' California house was. I ain't gon' lie, the rooms were nice as hell, but it wasn't worth the almost $400 per room per night that I paid. I mean, it had a living area and great views, so I guess I couldn't complain.

"So, Rojas wants us to meet him at his house tomorrow morning, but tonight he wants to welcome us to L.A. with an all-expense paid night at the OHM nightclub, and niggas, he paid for table service for the night, so dress to impress and I'll meet y'all downstairs later on. Have fun gentlemen, and welcome to L.A," Eric was speaking to us like this was his city and we were just visiting.

"Eric, ain't you from Chi-town, my nigga?" I asked, confused as to why he was talking to us like that.

"Nigga, I come to L.A. a lot; this y'all nigga first time, I'm just tryna show y'all muthafuckas a little hospitality but fuck it. I'll take that shit back," he snickered.

"Now that's the muthafucka I know," I laughed.

"Nigga, just meet me in the lobby at ten. I got some shit to do today." He left the room.

"So what the fuck we gon' do today, nigga?" Loco asked.

"Shit, we gon' check out L.A. and do some shopping and shit, might as well," I replied.

After calling Venus and Kay Kay to let them know we made it safely, we headed out of the hotel to see what L.A. was all about.

"Yo, these bitches out here fat as fuck. I might need to see what the fuck they working with," Loco said, looking around at all the fine ass bitches walking the streets.

"Yeah nigga, do that and Kay Kay will cut yo ass." I had to remind that nigga that he was dealing with a crazy ass bitch.

"Man fuck, you right; why in the hell did I come here in a relationship?" He shook his head.

"Shiiid, my ass married, so how the fuck y'all niggas think I feel right now?" Smoke asked, looking pissed. Me and Loco started laughing like shit.

After checking out the sights, eating, and shopping like we was some got damn stars, we went back to the hotel to rest up for our night.

****

The OHM club was lit as fuck. The music cranked, the crowd was hyped, and the table service was extraordinary. The mocha couches they had in the lounge area were comfortable as hell. Loco's ass was in there acting like a child; he kept changing the color of the lights on the table since you could change them to any color you want.

"Man, do every bitch in here wanna look like a fuckin' Kardashian or something?" Smoke asked, looking around at all the bitches in the club.

"Man, this is L.A.; some of them bitches might actually be niggas," Eric said.

"Fuck that, I'll put a bullet in a nigga's head quick as shit if he try to pull that fuckery shit on me." Loco was serious as shit.

After getting a few drinks in our system, I was ready to find some bitches to chill with. I went out on the dance floor and pulled a couple of bad bitches—and yes, I made sure they were real bitches. I brought them over to the lounge. The red bone was on me, sitting on my lap and shit and feeling on a niggas dick. I ain't gon' lie, I was all over her ass too. To tell the truth, all of us except Eric took a bitch back to the room with us. I didn't know about anybody else, but I fucked the shit outta the bitch I had with me. I had to admit, I loved L.A.

"Man Loco, you better hope Kay Kay don't find out what you did last night or your ass gon' be fucked up," I teased him as I took a sip of my orange juice.

"Shiiid nigga, don't act like Venus ain't gonna fuck yo ass up; shit nigga, or Raquel." He shook his head laughing.

"Fuck Raquel, she ain't my bitch. I don't stick my dick in her no more!" I snapped. I was pissed with the mentioning of her name.

My phone started ringing, and it was Eric telling us that the cars were downstairs to take us to Rojas' house. We got our shit and hurried downstairs. I was ready to talk to Rojas so I could find out what the fuck was going on, and handle my business. I wanted Frank and Maurice dead like yesterday.

We pulled up to this big ass house on 20th Street in Santa Monica; it reminded me of a mini version of Sosa's house from the movie Scarface.

Two big strong ass Spanish muthafuckas searched us before letting us into the house. The floors in the foyer and walkway were marble, and the walls were painted in a light tan. The strong nigga led us down the hallway and out the door to a patio overlooking the pool.

"Bienvenida a California, welcome to California," an averaged-sized, medium build Spanish guy said as he got up and walked over to us.

"Eric, how you been? How is Pharaoh? I am sorry to hear about Con; he was a good man," he spoke with a heavy Spanish accent as he shook Eric's hand.

"Juan Rojas, this is Adonis Thompson," Eric introduced us.

"Sí Adonis, bienvenida a mi casa en Santa Monica," he said, shaking my hand.

"Gracias, tienes una casa hermosa," I replied.

"¿Hablas a Español?" he asked.

"Muy poco," I replied, using my fingers to show a little bit.

"Oh, very little huh? Well, if you think this home is beautiful, it's nothing compared to my home in Colombia; come, let's sit and talk." He led us over to the table.

I had Loco and Smoke to join Tony and Sam at the table behind us.

"Gracias, Valentina," Rojas thanked the maid for bringing us drinks.

"Now Adonis, tell me about this Maurice and what deal he says we made?" he questioned.

"He said that you was offering $25,000 a kilo of cocaine, $4,500 a pound of loud, $1,000 a pound of regular weed, and $125,000 a kilo of heroin.

"BULLSHIT!" he shouted, banging his fist on the table.

He started speaking in Spanish so fast that I couldn't make out nothing but a few obscenities.

"I never deal with Maurice; we met one time and I didn't trust him, so I said no deal. I don't offer deals like that; I will never cut my prices that much," he informed me.

"This so-called deal got my brother Lavelle killed. Maurice lied about the deal and made it like my brother was stealing. I need to know everything." I needed Rojas to tell me everything that happened when he met with Maurice.

"I liked Lavelle. I wanted to meet with him. I hear on the streets he is loyal; I like loyal. Maurice said you brother didn't want to meet, so I said no deal." I could feel my anger rise. My heavy breathing, tight face, and flared nose must have shown Rojas exactly what I was thinking.

"Maurice lied to me too?" he asked. I nodded my head.

"No one lies to Rojas; Maurice will pay with his life," he said again, banging his fist on the table.

"Oh, I intend on taking his life," I assured. "I got information, but I need to have my own operation started before I carry out my plans; that's why I want a deal with you, and I am prepared right now to pay whatever price you have to offer," I added.

Rojas sat back in his seat twirling his thick mustache, thinking.

"Oh, here's what I do for you. I give you the deal Maurice lied about, on one condition. You bring me his head; after that, if I like your business, keep the deal." He stuck his hand out to shake on it.

I felt relieved. I signaled Loco to bring in the bags of money. Rojas counted the money in his counter, then told his guy to bring the merch. Knowing we would never get through customs with the merch, Rojas offered us the use of his private plane. I was ready to leave right then and there; it was time for me to put my plan into action.

Raquel

"Yes baby, fuck me harder," I moaned as my man was pounding my pussy hard and deep; I was loving the feeling of his dick filling up my walls.

"Do that nigga fuck you like this?" he grunted, grabbing my waist and pulling me back on his pole. "Do you let that nigga cum in this pussy while my baby in yo stomach?" he asked.

"NOOO," I groaned. "I don't fuck him no more; this yo pussy," I whined, throwing my ass back. "Gimme that dick, baby; cum in this pussy," I moaned. He sped up his pace as I continued fuckin' the shit outta of him.

"FUCK THAT NIGGA!" I shouted as he released inside me.

He laid back on the bed, and I laid my head on his chest, tryna catch my breath.

"I can't wait 'til all this is over and we can be together," I said, rubbing on his chest.

"Soon baby, I promise." He kissed me on the lips.

"How's my lil' man doing? I hate that I can't be there with you," he said.

"I know, but I'm only a few months; you don't even know if it's a boy," I chuckled.

"I say it's a boy." He rubbed my stomach.

"You figure out how you gonna get rid of that bitch?" I asked.

"Yeah, I have a kidnapping set up. I got eyes on her and know her every move; she will be gone sooner than you know," he told me.

"Thank you, baby; the sooner I can get rid of her, the sooner I can get his mind back focused on me, then you can handle yo business and take his ass out," I smiled at the thought of Adonis being dead. I hated him with a passion.

"Well, you know I have to go now; no matter how much I love fuckin' you in his bed." He got up, kissed me, and got dressed.

"I love you." He kissed me again before leaving.

I was glad Adonis was wherever he was at. I got to spend the whole night and morning making love to my real man. I snatched the sheets off of the bed and throw them into the washing machine, then I went to take a shower. After getting out of the shower, I changed the sheets on the bed and went to cook myself some lunch. I heard my phone start ringing, so I rushed up the steps to answer it.

"Hello," I answered.

"Why you outta breath?" he asked. It was my baby.

A mile-wide smile grew on my face. "You miss me already?" I asked, twirling my hair and biting down on my bottom lip.

"Yeah, I miss you," he said.

"I miss you too, and our baby misses you too; he been tearing my stomach apart," I giggled.

"What the fuck you just say?" Adonis voice startled me, making me jump and quickly hang up the phone.

I didn't see or hear him come in. I was so wrapped up in my conversation that I didn't see him standing in the doorway.

"B-b-baby, w-w-what you talking about?" I asked, stuttering and afraid that he heard what I said.

"Bitch, don't try to play dumb! Who the hell was you talking to telling them that you and their baby miss them? You know what? I don't give a fuck, but now I know yo hoe ass carrying another niggas seed; that's enough for me. Get the fuck outta my house," he spoke in a calm tone as if he really didn't care.

"Adonis, this is yo baby, I swear," I lied, hoping he would fall for the fake tears that came down my face.

"Nice try, but I heard everything; now, I'm gonna tell you one last time before I murk you and yo unborn bastard child." I could see hate in his eyes.

I hurried around the room, packing my stuff without saying word.

"Venus, the bitch was lying; she ain't having my baby," I heard him on the phone. He was sitting on the bed talking to her on speaker.

"Adonis, what the hell you talking about?" she asked.

"Raquel; this dumb bitch been fuckin' another nigga the whole time. Baby, you know what this means. I'm coming home, baby; we can be together." This nigga sounded happy as shit. Little did he know, his precious Venus would be gone before he could get warm in her bed.

"Adonis, look; slow down, I'm not following you," she said, sounding confused.

"Look, when this bitch leaves, I'll be there. I love you, Venus, and I promise I will make everything right." He ended the call and sat silent on the bed, watching me pack all my things and pointing out when I missed something. He didn't even help me take all my stuff to my car.

"FUCK YOU, ADONIS! YOU GON' GET YOURS! I PROMISE!" I yelled as I pulled out of his driveway.

"Hey baby, you ok? Did that nigga hear our conversation? Baby, did he hurt you?" He was throwing out questions before I could answer.

"Slow down, baby; he didn't hurt me, but he heard everything and kicked me out. He called that bitch and told her they can be together. I want to make his life a living hell; how soon can you set up the kidnapping?" I was rambling just like he was, pissed off.

"Tomorrow," he answered.

"Good, do it," I insisted. I hung up and headed to his house with a big smile on my face.

Venus

Adonis' phone call had my mind boggled; was he saying that Raquel was lying about being pregnant? He was talking with so much excitement that I couldn't hear everything he was saying. I paced the floor over and over again, racking my brain and tryna make sense of all this, but no matter how hard I think, I still can't figure it out. I hear a car approach and peek out of the window, but it wasn't Adonis. The car stopped in front of my house and sat there for a few minutes like they were looking for an address or something. I stepped back behind the curtain and watched. Suddenly, the car pulled off. I didn't think nothing of it before, but I had seen that car several times now, or maybe it was a car kind of like it; I couldn't really tell.

I sat down by the window to keep an eye out for Adonis. He was taking longer than I thought. I noticed that the car circled the block and parked a few houses down and turned off the lights. I waited to see who get out of it, but I really couldn't see. I squinted my eyes tryna get a good view, but then Adonis pulled up. I opened the door and stepped out onto the porch, waiting for him to approach.

"Adonis, did you notice a black car lurking around here?" I asked as I glanced down the street.

"Naw why?" he asked, concerned.

"I noticed it before, and I saw it again tonight; it was just parked a few houses down, but not I don't see it," I explained.

He grabbed me by my shoulders and led me into the house.

"You want me to get someone on it?" he looked at me with raised brows waiting for my response.

"No, that's ok, maybe it's nothing," I replied.

We walked into the living room and sat down.

"Now tell me what you was talking about," I told him, wanting to know what the phone call was about.

"Ok, you know that I was supposed to come home tomorrow. I told her the same thing, but business was handled quicker than I thought, and Rojas let us take his private plane so we got in today. You following me?" he asked, noticing the confused look I had.

I had no idea what business he had in California or why he was meeting with Rojas, whoever he is, but I nodded my head yes so he could continue telling me about Raquel.

"Well, I came in the house and went straight to the room. I heard her on the phone asking somebody if they missed her, so naturally I listened at the door. That's when I heard her say that she and their baby missed him too." I was flabbergasted.

"Are you sure she was saying the baby was someone else's?" I asked.

"Vee, I know what I heard, and the look she had on her face when I said something confirmed it. She looked like she seen a ghost." He grabbed my shoulders and looked me in the eyes. "Venus, she's not having my baby; she's outta our lives for good. We can work on getting our family back together," he assured.

I was still sitting there frozen in disbelief.

"Is this real?" I asked with a low voice.

"Baby, it's real, don't you want this?" he inquired with a distorted face.

"Yes I do, but I really can't take another cycle of trying to make us work, only to have something come along and fuck it up for me. I can't take another heartbreak from you, Adonis; it kills me," I had to address my concern.

"I promise Venus, I will never hurt you again; when you hurt, I hurt even if it don't seem like it. We can take it slow if you want, start over, just tell me what you want and it's done," he said.

"I do want to rebuild our relationship, and I do feel like we should take it slow just to be sure that we get it right this time, because I swear this is your last chance," I spoke truthfully from the heart.

He pulled me into an embrace, then kissed me.

"Do this mean no sex?" he asked.

"Not tonight," I laughed.

"That's cool; like I said, whatever you want." He kissed me again.

We went upstairs and got into bed. I turned on my side with my back to him; he wrapped his arm around my waist and buried his head in my back.

"Damn, I missed this." He whispered.

"I did too." I replied.

Adonis has always slept with me like that, and it wasn't easy sleeping alone without having his head buried in my back and his arm around me, so I kind of understood why it was easy for him to have Raquel staying with him. I still held a little resentment toward him for allowing another woman to take my place, but I would eventually get over it.

I was awakened by Adonis talking on the phone; he was telling somebody that his plan would be carried out tonight. I knew it had to have something to do with making Frank pay for Lavelle's death. He was hell bent on revenge, and I didn't like that. He was putting his life as well as ours at risk. I decided to mind my business and go shower; we could discuss letting shit go later.

On my way to work, I noticed the same black car following me a few cars behind; it was starting to worry me 'cause it could be the feds after Adonis, or even worse—it could be a hit. No, if it was a hit, they would have killed me by now, so my guess was that it was the feds. That thought put my mind at ease 'cause Lavelle taught Adonis how to keep his shit clean and to never stash his shit in the house, or keep more that he needed on his person; since he took over Lavelle's business, he had been more focused on turning the strip club into a nightclub, and not so much of the drug dealing.

I pulled up to the building just as Kay Kay was getting out of her new Lexus. She had on her shades, a fresh weave, and she was dressed to kill. Loco brought her some outfits from California; he said Adonis brought me and Harmony a bunch of shit too, but I guess with everything that happened last night, he forgot to give them to me.

"Girl, look at you looking like money," I boasted, getting out of the car.

"Yes, snatched honey!" she bragged, giving me her best model walk. We both laughed as she walked over to me and gave me a big hug.

"So, you ready to work close to Pierre again?" she asked.

"As long as he can be mature, I'm fine," I replied as we headed into the building.

"Kaylee, Venus, how are you two beautiful women doing today?" Pierre asked with a sexy ass smile on his face.

"I'm great, Pierre; how are you?" Kay Kay replied.

Pierre looked me dead in the eye "How have you been, Venus?" His sexy look and voice made me blush.

"I been good, Pierre; thanks for asking." I held his gaze for a few minutes, then turned away.

Kay Kay was looking at me with raised brows "He still want you girl, and from the looks of it, you want him too," she stated.

"Kaylee, I am pregnant with Adonis' child and we are working on our relationship, so me wanting Pierre is not a non-factor." I walked past her, went to the table, and pulled out my laptop with the new designs on it.

Kay Kay joined me and Pierre at the table, and we went about our day as professional as we could be, considering the fact that the three of us often clown around. Kay Kay thought that we should go to New York for fashion week this year to try to get advice and pointers from other designers. I thought it was a great idea, and possibly a huge opportunity for us. The only thing that was holding me back from doing that was I'd be big and pregnant by that time.

"Vee Vee, this could be a huge deal for us," she whined, stomping her foot like a child.

"I know, but maybe we can go next year, or you can go by yourself," I shrugged my shoulder.

She let out a sigh, turned her chair around, and folded her arms on the table pouting.

"Really Kay Kay, now you gon' act like Harmony when she don't get her way?" I mushed the side of her head.

"Seriously Venus, look at these new designs; they're innovative and really fashion forward. I think we could really build our brand if we had the proper connections, and what better way to do that than to go to fashion week? I mean yes, I can go by myself, but you can sell us the best. You have a certain way about you that makes people pay attention to you. I need you there," she stressed.

"I can fill in for Venus; with my charm and good looks, I can get people to listen," Pierre chimed in.

"I think that's a great idea; you, Pierre, and a model or two wearing our fashions. I think it will work," I agreed.

"Yeah Venus, but they are gonna want to meet you," she badgered.

"Well if they do, we can FaceTime or something, Kay Kay. We can work this out, then if we have anybody interested, we can set up meetings for after the baby is born," I said.

"She's right, Kay Kay; we can do this," Pierre concurred.

After a few more minutes of back and forth between the three of us, she finally agreed to go with Pierre and two of our best models; they were only going to attend the open to the public show, but I was hoping that they could get insight on what was need to be a part of the show and show our designs. Pierre got right to finding out how to get the tickets so all the arrangements could be made ahead of time.

I noticed that car again as I was driving home. I called Adonis and gave him the license plate number so that he could try to find out who it was; it was really starting to creep me out. He told me to get Harmony and go to his mother's house for the night. He had something to do and needed to feel like I was safe until he found out who it was. He told me not to worry about going home and getting clothes; he would come over with everything we needed. I agreed and followed his instructions. I noticed the car followed me until we entered his mother's neighborhood. I didn't know what this was about, but I hoped Adonis got to the bottom of it real soon. I had a strange feeling about this.

Adonis

I was pissed about Venus being followed. I knew Frank got the message that I was coming for him; if not, he should be. I just knew that his ass bet not have anybody following my girl. I took the piece of paper that I wrote the tag number on, then called Beans and told him I needed information on that car ASAP. I then called Loco and Smoke to tell them to meet me tonight at the spot. It was time to make sure Frank heard my message loud and clear.

The knocking on the door interrupted my conversation with Loco. I ended the call, then told the contractor to come in. The contractor needed me to check out the wall and the stripper pole that they knocked down; he needed me to sign off saying that it met my standards. We also went over where and how I wanted the lighting as well as the paint choices. I was pleased with the progress the contractors made so far and signed off on the form.

After the workers left, I got my things together and headed to the meeting spot. Venus and Harmony's picture flashed on my screen, alerting me that Venus was calling. I hit the button to allow the call to come through the speakers.

"Yeah, baby," I answered.

"Yeah, I just was telling you that I was at your moms; will you be here for dinner or should I put it up for you?" she asked.

I had to smile; she always made sure that I was taken care of. I missed that so much.

"Just put me up some. I don't know what time I will be there, but when I get there you better be ready for me to dig in those guts," I replied.

"Whatever you say, sir," she giggled, then snorted. I missed that too.

Loco and Smoke were already waiting for me at the spot when I arrived. Loco was checking the ammo making sure we had everything that we needed to handle our business.

"Yo, boss what's the plan?" Smoked asked.

"We got to make this in and out, kill everyone in the houses, take all their stash, then burn the bitch down," I spoke with authority as I ran down my plan.

"So we thieves now?" Loco asked, grabbing bags for the stash.

"We whatever the fuck we need to be to get the shit done," I replied.

My plan is to hit this nigga's major money makers to make his ass go come for me. Frank played no games when it came to his money, and I played no games when it came to getting revenge for my brother. He wanted to lay low and act like he gave a shit about Lavelle, then I was gonna fuck up everything he has until he wanted to retaliate. I'd get

Ty Leese Javeh

my war and could take out him and his whole entire empire.

"So what spot we hittin' tonight?" Smoke asked.

"Nigga, we hittin" all of them," I stated.

"So, we about to hit all three of this nigga's biggest traps in one night?" Loco inquired as he clapped his hands.

"That's right, Loco; we about to put in work. Y'all niggas ready for this?" I looked back and forth between Loco and Smoke.

"Nigga, do you really have to ask me some dumb shit like that?" Loco responded with a distorted look.

We got suited up, got in the black SUV Smoke provided for us, and headed to Benning Road to hit up the first trap.

"Aight Loco, go do what you do, nigga; let us know what's going on," I instructed.

Loco got out the car and went to check shit out. I needed to know how many niggas was inside and who was around. Loco was a pro at peepin' shit out when we was about to put in work. I didn't know how his ass dipped in and out unnoticed, but whatever it was worked. He got back into the car and gave us the information we needed to do what we had to do.

"Aight, it's four niggas inside; they strapped, but we can get them before they can pull out, and it's one nigga sitting on the back porch smoking; I got him. It's a fiend out there lurking around; I'll snatch his ass up and make him get us in the house, then we can handle our business and get the fuck out," he informed us.

Loco got out the car and went to take care of the nigga in the back, and snatch up the dope fiend so we could do what we do. A few minutes later, he came back to the car with the nigga at gunpoint.

"What's yo name, nigga?" I asked.

"M-Mike," he stuttered.

"Ok Mike, if you follow our instructions carefully, you won't get hurt you. Feel me?" He nodded yes. We took the nigga to the door, and I told him to take a deep breath and act normal.

"If you try anything stupid, I will cut your limbs off before putting a bullet in yo skull, you got me?" I looked at this nigga with death in my eyes. He nodded yes, then proceeded to knock on the door.

"Who the fuck is it?" a nigga yelled from the other side of the door tryna sound tough.

"It's Mike, I need something," he answered, sounding as normal as he could with a gun pointed at his head.

I heard the nigga unlock several locks on the door; we cocked our guns and made sure our silencers were secure. The nigga opened the door, and we pushed our way in.

Pew! Pew! Pew! Pew!

We murked all four of them muthafuckas before they could pull out. Loco opened the door and dragged the nigga he killed on the back porch into the house, and put him next to the other niggas. He was repeatedly stabbed in the neck.

"Damn Loco, you tried to take the bitch ass nigga's head off?" I laughed.

"Shiiid, he lucky I didn't," he replied.

We hurried and snatched up everything they had stashed in the house.

"What we gon' do with this scary ass muthafucka?" Loco asked, pointing at Mike, who was curled up in the corner shaking and shit.

"Kill him," I replied, shrugging my shoulders.

Pew! Pew!

Loco put two bullets in his dome. Smoke came out of the kitchen and informed us that he finished cutting the gas line on the stove. We ran out the back door. Smoke lit a book of matches and tossed it inside. It didn't take long before the house was in flames. We dipped through the bushes and made our way to the SUV, and got the hell from around there.

"Yeah, that's the type of shit I'm talkin' about," Loco exploded with joy. "Kill everything movin', take everything in there, and dip the fuck out," he continued.

"Nigga, calm yo crazy as down," I laughed.

I looked back at the nigga as he mumbled *rest in peace niggas* and kissed his cross. I would never understand that, but that was his thing just like mine was to shower, fuck, and eat.

We pulled up to the next trap on Southern Avenue and repeated our actions, only this one was much easier; it was some young dumb niggas, so we kicked the door in to gain access.

The third and final trap was on Brightseat Road in Landover, Maryland. That one was the hardest. Loco did his thing and scooped out the place, and came back to the car.

"I don't know about this shit, nigga; it's like 10 deep in there. Muthafuckas all standing around drinking and smoking while they playing cards. We might have to say fuck it to this one," he said.

"Naw nigga, I came prepared." I reached in the back and pulled out the other bag. I opened it and gave them niggas a gas mask, then I grabbed the smoke bombs.

"Loco, you go to the back; me and Smoke gon' go to the front. Shoot a blank text to my phone when you in position; when you hear us kick the door in, you do the same and throw all the smoke bombs. They cant's see us, but we can see them; kill everybody." I ordered.

BOOM!

Smoke kicked in the door in with one kick. We tossed in the smoke bombs.

"WHAT THE FUCK!" I heard a nigga shout.

BOOM!

Loco kicked the back door and tossed in the smoke bombs.

As smoke filled the house, Loco held down the back and I held down the front, killing anybody that tried to run out. Smoke went upstairs to make sure no one else was in the house. When the smoke downstairs cleared up some, there was four niggas crouched behind the couches with their guns drawn. I looked at Loco and he shook his head.

Pew! Pew! Pew! Pew!

We both took out two apiece; when he informed us that it was clear, we grabbed the stash, then Loco set the sofas on fire and Smoke set the curtains on fire.

We got back to our spot and counted the money and the merch; all together, we got over a quarter of a million dollars.

"Oh shit, I know Frank gonna come after us now." Smoke laughed.

"Yeah, and when he do, we gon' be ready. I made a call earlier and got extra help on the way." I knew this was only the beginning, and when Frank retaliated, he was gon' come hard.

After stashing our shit, we parted ways. I called Venus to make sure she was good, then I went home, took a shower, grabbed the stuff I brought Venus and Harmony from Cali, then headed to my mother's house so I could complete my ritual. I already took a shower, now the only other things I needed to complete my night is pussy and food.

I hit up Beans as I was driving up the highway. I wanted to know if he had any information on that car that was following Venus.

"The car belongs to an Alexia Martin." he informed.

"Who the hell is that?" I asked puzzled.

"I don't know, but that' not all. It seems that the tags are registered to a red Nissan Maxima, and the car you described is a black Buick, so it doesn't match."

I thanked him and we ended the call. I was more confused now. Who the fuck was Alexia Martin, and why in the hell was Venus being followed? I had no answers to any of those questions, but I knew it was no way in hell I was going to Detroit until this shit was handled and I knew Venus was safe.

Venus

I was almost finished braiding Harmony's hair when Adonis came in with a bunch of shopping bags from expensive stores.

"Hi, Daddy." Harmony spoke, waving her hands.

"Hey baby, you getting yo hair all pretty for daddy?" He walked over to her and kissed her forehead. She giggled.

"What you got in the bags, Daddy?" she asked in a high-pitched tone, excited as if she already knew he brought her something.

"I got some stuff for you and mommy." he answered as he stroked my hair.

"How you doing?" he asked, kissing me on the top of my head.

"I'm fine." I replied.

He sat on the bed directly behind me and slid his hand under my ass.

"Didn't I tell you to be ready for me when I got home?" he whispered in my ear as he slid his finger under my shorts.

"Adonis, stop." I whispered, hoping Harmony wasn't hearing us.

I elbowed him and tried to shift to make him remove his fingers. He moved closer to me and started rubbing on my clit. I tried to sit still like I wasn't bothered by him fondling me. I finished the last braid and told Harmony to go take a bath.

"Can I see what Daddy got me first?" she asked, jumping up and down.

"No, you can go ask grandma if you can take a bubble bath in her big ole tub while daddy talk to mommy about something." he told her.

"Ok, Daddy." she pouted, then ran out of the room.

Adonis got up, then closed and locked the door.

"When I tell you to be ready, I mean that shit." he said as he snatched me off of the bed.

"Adonis, I said we can take it slow." I tried to push him away.

"I'll take it slow." He pulled me into a kiss. He pulled down my shorts and underwear, then pulled off his pants.

"Sorry, I can't be slow. Harmony gon' be at the door soon wanting to see her stuff." He pushed me down until I was bent over the bed, then grabbed my hips and thrust inside of me. He was hittin' me fast as shit, going deeper and deeper with each stroke.

"Adonis, damn, slow down." I groaned, but of course he didn't listen; in fact, he started going faster.

My body started trembling; he gripped me tighter and thrust deeper. I almost screamed, but I buried my face in the bed. He grabbed my shoulders and pulled me back to him as I bounced my ass on his dick. I rolled my hips, matching his rhythm, and the trembles in my body got stronger and stronger. His heavy breathing let me know that he was about to bust, so I threw my ass back, making sure to slide up and down his pole. He gripped my hips and held me in place as I felt his rod pulsating and his warm nut flowing inside of me.

"Damn, for a quickie, that shit was amazing." he breathed. "What you cook?" he asked.

"Lasagna, garlic bread, and salad." I replied.

"Hell yeah, a nigga hungry as fuck." he rubbed his stomach.

I shook my head. "Your food is in a container in the microwave, and your salad is in a container in the fridge." He kissed me, then slapped my ass

"You always looking out for me." He winked, then headed downstairs.

I started going through the bags to see what he brought me and Harmony. A few minutes later, Harmony ran into the room, eager to see her new clothes. We both were excited and started holding the clothes against our bodies and looking in the mirror.

"Mommy, what is goooccccii?" she asked, looking confused while holding up a Gucci dress.

I laughed. "It's Gucci, baby." I picked up the same dress for a cute little mommy and me look.

"Mommy, we gon' be twins." she beamed.

"Yep, but you will never look like mommy 'cause you look exactly like daddy," Adonis said from the doorway. He walked over and picked her up. "Daddy loves you so much."

He twirled her around in the air. It reminded me of the father and daughter I saw at the park the day of the funeral. I knew he missed her, but the way he was gazing so lovingly at her stamped it for me. I was glad to have my family back together; my only hope was that we could stay together now.

"Harmony, take you new clothes in your room and daddy will come and tuck you in bed in a few minutes, ok?" I said.

She grabbed her bags and ran into her bedroom. I closed the door.

"Adonis, I need to tell you something." My tone was serious as I sat him on the bed.

"What?" he replied.

"Sabrinae and her boyfriend are in town, and I invited them over tomorrow." I said.

"What, why would you do that?" Just like I knew he would, he flew off the handle.

"I don't want to see her, I don't even know the girl, and you invited her here without my permission and with shit going on. What the fuck is wrong with you?" He was furious.

"What the fuck is wrong with you? You mad at the world right now, fine, but she's your sister and she had nothing to do with what your father did. She wasn't even born, so you can't take it out on her."

"I can take it out on anybody I want to." he snapped.

"That's not how the world works, Adonis." I snapped back.

"My world do." He tried walking past me, but I grabbed his shirt.

"Get over yourself, Adonis; she will be here tomorrow evening and you will be nice, simple as that." I stated.

"She can come, but I won't be here." He was being so stubborn, and I wanted to slap some sense in his ass.

"Adonis." his mother called him from the door.

"Come in, ma." I called out.

She walked into the room and sat on the bed, pulling him down with her.

"Look, I've forgiven your father and it's ok if you didn't, but Sabrinae is not responsible for his actions; neither are you. She's your sister, and you need to get to know her; now, she will be here tomorrow and so will you. No ifs, ands, or buts about it. That's my final word." Before he could respond, she got up and left the room.

He looked at me with narrowed eyes and a scowl on his face, but I didn't care; he needed to get to know his sister.

"I'm going to put Harmony in the bed." He stormed out of the room.

I climbed in bed, flicking the channels on the TV.

When he came back into the room, he apologized for snapping on me, then asked where was his sister staying. I gave him the information and he said that he only wanted to see her first; he would meet her husband after they talked. I was ok with that; it was a start.

The next day, I was out running some errands and I noticed that same car was following me everywhere. I called Adonis and told him; he was pissed off, but he told me to act normal and keep running my errands until he called me back. He told me to stay in areas where there were a lot of people. I did what I was instructed to do.

Loco

When Adonis got the call from Venus about being followed again, we figured that it was somebody trying to learn her routine 'cause the feds would have picked her up already. The only reason to study a person's daily routine was if you were planning on kidnapping that person.

"Adonis, tell her to keep doing what she doing and you gon' call her back. I got a plan." I suggested.

He instructed her to keep runnin' her errands and stay in areas where there was lots of people. She agreed, and he ended the call.

"You thinking what I'm thinking?" he questioned.

"Yeah, somebody tryna snatch her, and I'm about to dead a nigga." I replied.

I made a call to my nigga Dex that worked as an attendant at the parking garage on I Street. He told me that it was mostly empty, and if I needed a dark area and with no cameras, he would tell me where to go. Me and Adonis strapped up and hurried to the garage. I told him to call Venus and make sure she was still being followed; she was.

We got to the garage and Dex showed us the perfect spot to handle business. We got in position and I called Venus.

"Look, I want you to go to the parking garage on I Street; my man Dex is in the booth, but he gonna open the gate right before you get here and duck down, so whoever following you won't see him; stay on the phone on speaker, and we will guide you straight to us." I instructed.

"Baby, we got you; don't be scared, and act as normal as you can," Adonis spoke into the phone.

"Adonis, I'm not scared. I know you and Loco got me." she replied.

She stayed on the phone silent until she was almost at the garage. I hit up Dex and told him she was turning the corner, and he let the gate up and ducked down.

"Ok Venus, I want you to go to the ground floor to the dark area in the back, park the car, and act like you are getting stuff out. You won't see me and Adonis, but we are right there with eyes on you. Ok? And don't be nervous." I directed her.

Adonis hid behind the truck she was to park next to and I hid behind the wall. Venus pulled into the parking space and did exactly what I told her to do. She looked and acted natural. I noticed the black car follow her in with the lights out, backing into the space closest to the door, but still close to her. As she started walking past the car, the door opened and somebody jumped out and started walking behind her in a fast pace. Adonis crouched down and made his way over to the car. Venus reached for the door and the nigga grabbed her from behind, placing his hand over her mouth. She elbowed him and stomped on his foot so her heel could poke him, then she ran and ducked behind the car. I stepped from behind the wall and put the gun to the back of his head.

"If you value yo life, muthafucka, you would tell me who the fuck you working for." I said. The nigga looked in the direction of the car.

The person in the car started it up; Adonis got in the car with his gun pointed at the nigga temple.

"You ain't going nowhere." he stated.

"Baby, you ok?" he called out.

Venus came from behind the truck; she was visibly shaken. I hit the nigga in the back of his head with the butt of my gun, knocking him out, then I grabbed Venus and took her over to the car. I opened the driver's side door and pointed my gun at his temple so Adonis could go tend to Venus.

"You ok?" he asked, hugging her tightly.

"Yeah, but that was scary as hell; somebody tryna kidnap me?" She was still trembling.

"It appears that way." he answered.

"Who? Why?" She was asking questions that he couldn't answer.

He told her to go to his mother's house and stay there. She got in the car and left. Me and Adonis turned out attention to the two punk ass niggas that tried to snatch her.

"Get yo punk ass up!" Adonis shouted, stomping on the muthafucka that was knocked out. "Loco, let's take these niggas to the warehouse." He dragged the nigga off the ground and tossed him in the back seat.

"Drive, muthafucka." I commanded the driver.

He started the car and left out of the garage. I stopped at the booth and tossed Dex a stack, and headed to the warehouse so we could have some fun with these niggas.

****

We got to the warehouse and parked inside; we dragged the niggas out of the car and strung them up so they were hanging from the ceiling. They were both scared as hell, trembling like they were freezing. I laughed.

"You armature ass niggas," I shook my head. "Man the fuck up, lil' bitch!" I shouted in the muthafucka's face. His bottom lip was quivering as he started to speak.

"Man, we don't know nothin'." he said in a tremulous tone.

"What the fuck was you kidnapping my girl?" Adonis asked.

"I don't know, we were told to follow her and take her, and then they was gon' tell us where to drop her!" he exclaimed with tears in his eyes.

"Who is they?" Adonis asked. His voice was toneless as he questioned these niggas.

"Look, man my name is Anfernee and I got a family like you; please don't kill me." he begged, tryna make this shit personal like give a fuck about his fuckin' family.

Adonis nodded his head, then we started working these niggas bodies. Screaming in pain, the nigga Anfernee begged for us not to hit him no more.

"Then tell me what the fuck you know!" Adonis' voice boomed throughout the warehouse. I saw a look in his eyes that I'd never seen before; it was almost sadistic, as if he was enjoying what he was doing.

"So y'all stupid muthafuckas don't know who the fuck hired you, and you were willing to kidnap my girl, but want to beg me not to kill you 'cause you got a family." he burst out laughing, but it wasn't his normal laugh; it was more evil-sounding.

"You funny, my nigga." He walked over to the water hose and turned it on. He sprayed them both with cold water, making them soak and wet.

"Bring me the wires." he demanded.

I walked over to the table and got the wires. I flipped the switch to turn the electricity on. I passed him one set of wires and took the other set; shit, I wanted to have fun too.

"Please don't do this, man; we told you all we know." Anfernee begged, watching Adonis touch the wires together and cause them to spark.

"AAAAAHHHHHHH!" he yelled when Adonis stuck the wires on him.

He body was jerking so hard I thought he was gonna fall from the ceiling. It looked fun, so I did the same to the other nigga and watched him scream and jerk around, swinging from the ceiling. It's a good thing this warehouse was soundproof. We looked at each other and repeated our actions. One of the niggas shitted on himself.

"You nasty muthafucka." I said as I hosed the nigga down.

"Look man, I just know that this man's girl wanted your girl to be gone, I don't know why." the nigga that shitted on himself spoke in a brittle voice.

"These nigga telling the truth." Adonis said. "Cut them down, I got shit to do." he added.

I cut them down and the niggas' bodies hit the ground like a sack of potatoes. I knew they felt relieved, but little did they know, that was only the beginning. Adonis grabbed the metal bat and started beating the shit outta of one of the niggas. I could hear his bones breaking. I wanted in on the action but fuck a bat. I stomped down on the other nigga's legs over and over so hard that I broke them bitches.

"Damn nigga, that looks like fun." Adonis chuckled.

He dropped the bat and started stomping the nigga he was beating. We stomped and kicked these niggas every fuckin' where, knockin' teeth out and shit. Finally, Adonis grabbed his gun; that was my cue to grab mine and we put a couple bullets in their heads.

Adonis called the clean-up crew and we waited for them to arrive. I fired up a blunt and took a couple of puffs.

"Man, let me hit that shit." Adonis said, shocking the shit outta me.

"Nigga, you don't smoke." I replied.

"Well, I am today muthafucka." he chuckled.

I passed him the blunt and he took a toke; he choked, but continued to smoke.

"So what we gonna do about Detroit?" I asked as he passed me back the blunt.

"I have to meet my sister today, but we going to Detroit. I have to stop whatever the fuck Maurice got going on there. I'm serious about this shit. Frank probably the nigga that tried to snatch Venus in retaliation for his traps; his ass, along with his son, needs to be in the dirt ASAP." He took the blunt from my hand and took another pull.

"Adonis, you know I'm down for whatever we need to do; fuck them niggas, they need to die." I gave Adonis dap.

"Man, why the hell I didn't smoke before? This shit is relaxin' as hell." he laughed.

"Aye Loco, I need a huge favor. I need to go to my moms and get myself right. I'm staying there until I find a new house for my family; start fresh, you know. But anyway, can you get my sister from the Towne Place Suites on Ferry Avenue this evening and bring her to my mom's?"

"Yeah man, I got you; go home and get yourself together. You been dealin' with a lot lately. Relax a bit 'cause you don't know what type of convo you and your sis gon' have and you, my unstable nigga, needs to get yo mind right."

A few minutes later, the cleaning crew arrived and we headed out.

Kay Kay

Leaving Adonis' mother's house and thinking about Venus almost being kidnapped had my mind racing; that shit was fuckin' crazy. I was glad Adonis and Loco were there to stop them. Who would want to kidnap her, or follow her for that matter? One thing I could say about those two: don't fuck with their family. I know them niggas dead in the gutter somewhere.

I pulled up at the stoplight and sat back, waiting for the light to change. I was bobbin' my head to the music and chillin'. I looked over to the left and noticed Loco's truck sitting in the driveway of the Towne Place Suites.

What the fuck that nigga doing at a hotel? I thought to myself.

The light turned green, and I drove down the street and busted a U, and headed to the hotel. I called him and he didn't answer, so I shot him a text.

Me: *Where you at??????*

I waited for a response; when I didn't get one, I flipped the fuck out. I parked my car right next to his and got out.

"I can't believe this nigga at a hotel with a bitch. I told his ass not to play these type of games with me." I fumed to myself.

I dug through my purse until I found my blade. I took off my earrings and bracelet and went over to his truck. I slashed all four tires, but that wasn't enough for me. I started scratching it up. I busted out the front window, then sat on the top of the hood and waited. Him and that bitch had to come out sometime. I couldn't believe the dumb muthafucka didn't even put his alarm on.

I was sitting on top of the hood with my legs crossed, cleaning my nails with my blade. Loco rounded the corner with some dark-skinned bitch carrying her bag and shit.

"WHAT THE FUCK! KAY KAY, YOU CRAZY BITCH!" he yelled as he approached his truck.

He was enraged; his voice was loud like a foghorn as it boomed through the parking lot. I hopped off the hood of his truck just as pissed off as he was.

"What the fuck you doing here with this bitch? I told you not to fuckin' play these type of games with me." I raged as I rushed toward him ready to fight.

I swung on him and landed a few punches; he grabbed my wrists and yoked me up.

"You lost yo muthafuckin' mind, Kaylee. I been tryin' my hardest not to fuck you up, but you make it real fuckin' difficult." He pushed me away and headed toward his truck to assess the damage.

"Look, I don't know you but—" the girl started, but I shut her shit down real quick.

"Bitch, you don't wanna know me, trust me. Right now, you better stand there and shut the fuck up, and let me deal with my man before shit get ugly out here." I spat.

"Kay Kay, shut the fuck up and listen to me." Loco said as he snatched me away from the girl.

I slapped him. "I don't wanna hear shit you got to say, nigga!" I started back to my car, but Loco grabbed me by my throat and slammed me against the truck.

"I'm tryin' real hard, Kaylee." He was squeezing my throat and shaking me against the truck. I tried to swing on him, but my hits didn't faze him any.

"Either calm the fuck down and listen to me, or you can walk the fuck away but if you walk away, stay the fuck outta my life. I don't need this shit, you understand? Cause as much as I love yo crazy ass, I'll BURY yo ass before I let you treat me like a lil' bitch." The look in his eyes let me know that he was dead ass and wasn't playing games with my ass. He loosened up the grip he had around my neck.

"You ready to listen?" he asked.

"Fuck you, Loco."

He punched the glass outta his truck. I tried to move away from him but he yoked me back against the truck.

"Loco, please stop; people might be calling the police," the girl said in a softly spoken voice.

"I...DON'T...GIVE...A...FUCK!"   he shouted in a strangulated voice.

I ain't gon' lie, that nigga put fear in me; every time I tried to move away from him, he would slam me back against the truck.

"You gon' hear what the fuck I got to say!" he snapped as he pinned me against the side of the truck.

"Before you continue actin' crazy and I do something to you, understand this. I never in my life told a bitch I love her, and I'm tellin' you I love yo simple ass. I'm not about to fuck up what I got. You wanna know who this girl is while you out here threatening her and calling her out her name?" he questioned.

"Yeah nigga, who the fuck is she?" I rolled my neck and eyes.

"Sabrinae Thompson, Adonis' sister. I was picking her up for him." he replied in a calm voice.

I looked over at her and she waved at me, then a nigga came up to her and held her in his arms.

"What's goin' on? Are you alright?" he asked her.

"Yeah baby, this is Loco's girlfriend; she attacked him 'cause she thought he was cheating with me." she answered, looking dead at me.

I felt so stupid and to add insult to injury, she passed me the phone and Venus' voice came blurring through the speaker.

"Kaylee, what the fuck is wrong with you? Have you lost yo entire mind? That is Adonis' sister and she was coming over here to meet and talk to him for the first time, and yo ass out there actin' all crazy and shit—what the fuck is you doin'? You know everything that happened today, and you still wanna turn up on his ass and act like you don't got no muthafuckin' sense? Go the fuck on with that juvenile shit." she ranted.

"Venus, I'm sorry. I just spazzed out when I saw his truck and he didn't answer his phone." I spoke in a low voice, feelin' dumb as fuck. Loco reached in his truck and grabbed his cell off the seat. He passed it to me.

"I left my phone in the truck; I was only running in to get her." He walked over to her and who I now know was her boyfriend Mongoose, and apologized. I apologized to them as well, then I offered to pay for Loco's truck.

"Kaylee, don't insult me like that. I would never let you do that, but you are gon' pay for what you did, and you are gon' learn to trust me." he told me, then he gave me a quick peck on the lips.

"And you are gonna bring them over here." Venus' voice came through the phone; I forgot she was on speaker.

Sabrinae kissed Mongoose, then got in the back seat of my car. Loco took my keys and got into the driver's side, I didn't protest. I looked at him out of the side of my eye.

"You feel real stupid now, don't you?" I nodded my head yes.

"Girl, don't worry about it, I probably woulda did the same thing; shit, let me catch Mongoose with another bitch." Sabrinae started laughing. "Shit, I did one time and I hopped on the top of his car and beat it with a bat, yelling for him to come outside. I mean, I broke all the windows, dented the top and the hood all up, and they called the police on my ass. I didn't care; I was not going anywhere 'til he brought his ass outside. He did when he heard the sirens, but my baby got me outta there before the police came. I ain't never have a problem with him cheating again." We both started laughing.

Loco shook his head and said, "Let me find out all y'all crazy as fuck."

"Shiid nigga, your ass can't talk, out here talkin' bout as much as you love her you would bury her, and I can tell you meant that shit." she replied.

A few minutes later, we walked through Mrs. Thompson's door and she slapped me and Loco both in the head.

"What the hell wrong with you two out there actin' like fools?" Loco gon' throw me under the bus.

"It was her." he pointed at me.

"Boy, it was you too," she said "Y'all all crazy, including my son.

"What I do?" Adonis asked, sounding like a kid.

"Boy, do I need to make a list?" she shook her head, then hugged Sabrinae, then me and Loco. Adonis playfully mushed my head.

"Lil crazy ass." I playfully slapped him on the arm.

He walked over to Sabrinae and hugged her, then led her into the living room. Me and Loco decided that it was time for us to go home and give them privacy.

Loco was quiet as hell in the car. I didn't know if I should say anything to him 'cause I could see that he was still pissed. He picked up his phone, called somebody, and told them to go to his truck, then he called out the address. He got off the phone and continued to drive to my house in silence.

He walked into the house and went straight into the kitchen, grabbed his bottle out of the freezer, then went to the bedroom. A few minutes later, he called me to the room. He was sitting on the bed smoking a blunt. He motioned for me to sit down next to him. He took a pull of the blunt, then blew out the smoke.

"Do I make it hard for you to trust me?" he asked in a low, calm voice.

"It's hard for me to trust men period." I spoke truthfully.

"Why?" he asked.

I gave him a look that said *you should already know.*

"So, I got to pay the price for what other niggas did to you? I mean, I could have carried you and treated you the same way that I treated other women based on the shit these other bitches do, but I don't. I see you differently, even though you the craziest girl I ever been with." he smirked. "I told you I never told another girl that I love her; you the only one, and I try to show you every day. Real talk, if any other girl would have acted like you did tonight, I would have beat the dog shit outta her or worse—I might have killed her. I don't want that type of drama in my life. I have enough shit going on." he continued.

"I'm sorry, Orlando; really, I am," I apologized slightly above a whisper "I never felt for a man the way I feel for you, and it's like I'm waiting for you to fuck up." I spoke the truth.

"Ok, I would be lying if I tell you I wasn't tempted; shit, when we was in Cali, we were partying at this hot ass club, and bitches were everywhere. I mean, bad bitches. I took a girl back to the room with me and she was about to start sucking my dick…. but before she could even put her mouth on it, I thought of you and I made her ass leave. I couldn't cheat on you. I let the niggas assume I did but I didn't, I promise." He put his arm around my neck

"I didn't have to tell you that, but I want you to know that I will always be honest with you 'cause I love you." He kissed me passionately, then laid back on the bed, pulled me on top of him, and held me tightly. That night, after having sex, we feel asleep ass naked with me laying on top of him and his arms around my waist holding me tightly. I could finally say I trust him wholeheartedly.

One week later

Adonis

I've been building a relationship with my sister very well, and I'm glad Venus and my mom forced me to talk to her. I found out that even though Levar was a big part of her life, he wasn't that good of a father to her either. I guess once a piece of shit, always a piece of shit. I also learned that she goes to the University of Illinois at Chicago and plans on pledging. I wasn't too fond of her boyfriend Mongoose, though; he seemed like the average lil' knucklehead that wanted to be a street nigga, but he attended college with her so I could be all wrong.

Although I enjoyed my sister visiting every day, I was sick of staying at my mother's house. I was contemplating on going back home. Venus didn't feel safe going to her house, cause we was unsure if Frank was behind the kidnapping or not. She wasn't going back to my house because of one simple fact, I let Raquel live there with me. I had a realtor tryna find a house that I felt was good enough for our growing family, but she wasn't finding anything in the area that me and Venus wanted to be in. Since I took over Lavelle's business, I didn't want to be too far. Venus thought we should expand our area of interest, adding Bowie and Upper Marlboro to the list. I wasn't sure about that, but after the call I received from my security service informing me that my house was on fire, I had no choice but to expand the area of interest if I want to move quickly.

Me and Venus went to the house to see the damage; thank God my neighbors called the fire department and they were able to quickly put out the fire, so we didn't lose much. Everything inside smelled of smoke, but I didn't care. I planned on purchasing all new furniture anyway. The fire chief thought that it was arson, but he would have to investigate further before he could determine that.

Me and Venus packed as much of our clothes as we could 'cause I was leaving for Detroit later and didn't have time to go through everything.

On the way back to my mother's, I told Venus that I would call the realtor and tell her that we wanted to look into Bowie and Upper Marlboro, and that she would be meeting with her.

"What if I find a house and you not there to approve?" she asked.

"Look, take my mother with you and I trust that together, y'all will find a house that we would both love. I have to go to Detroit and handle my business." I replied.

"Ok Adonis, if that's what you want." she agreed.

When we got back to my mother's house, I called the realtor and gave her the same instructions that I gave Venus, then I packed my clothes.

"I know whatever you going to Detroit for has something to do with Frank," Venus stated as she watched me place the last few items in my bag.

"Why you say that?" I asked.

"Because, Adonis, I know you, and I know that Frank is behind Lavelle's death, and you're out for blood. I understand you got to do what you have to do; all I ask is for you to be safe." She walked over to me and gave me a light kiss.

"I'll be safe, I promise. I got you and my kids to come back home to." She smiled and wrapped her arms around my neck. She had a worried look on her face.

"Hey, don't worry. I know shit been going on lately, but trust that I got this; nothing is gonna happen to me or you." I embraced her tightly.

"I love you." she said in a low voice.

"I love you too Venus, and I'm coming home." I promised, then kissed her goodbye.

I called Loco and Smoke and told them I was on my way. I kissed Venus and Harmony good by one last time before leaving out the door.

****

We arrived at Detroit Metropolitan Airport around seven that evening, and as promised, Eric had three niggas waiting for us at the gate. After introducing ourselves, we went the Travel Lodge Ramulus Hotel. We decided not to go out that evening so we could rest and discuss our plan of action. I wanted to spend a few days getting to know the area, and keeping eyes on them niggas to learn their every move.

I found out that Maurice had a trap house in the Russell Woods area of Detroit; it was on Tyler Street off of Broadstreet Avenue. I noticed some niggas that frequented the house were actually runners going to reup, and every day at certain times, they would all meet at the trap. I planned to be at one of the meeting times, but first I needed one of the runners to get information from.

Loco and Smoke followed one of the niggas and found that Maurice took a page from my brother's book and had another house where the drug was stashed; I'm assuming like my brother, only certain people knew the location, so that told me that this lil' nigga was someone of importance. I decided that he was the one we was gonna break. I had Loco and two of the niggas Eric sent named D-Boy and Gutta stay on him. Me, Smoke, and Eric's nigga Loco—who I decided to call L so we won't get confused by the two crazy ass niggas—went to meet up with a connect that L knew to get us some weapons. After purchasing our guns and ammo, we waited for Loco to call and let us know the nigga was in the house.

About 30 minutes later, we got the call from Loco; he informed us that they had the nigga and his friend gagged and tied up in the house; we were on our way.

"I hope this shit goes smooth and easy." Smoke said, puffin' on a blunt.

"Nigga, that's up to these muthafuckas; it can go smooth or rough, depending on how they respond." I said.

"Shiiid, I'm the type of nigga that likes them to fake tough so I can break their bitch asses down." L smirked. He had a devilish-looking half-smile on his face, reminding me of my nigga Loco.

"Damn, is all muthafuckas named Loco crazy as fuck?" I asked jokingly.

"Fuck if I know, I just know I'm not the muthafucka to fuck with." he stated.

"Nigga, that's like askin' do all niggas named Smoke actually smoke." Smoke chuckled and choked on the blunt at the same damn time.

"Muthafucka, you said that shit while you puffin' on a jay; nigga, shut yo simple ass up." I laughed.

We arrived at the house, and I got the bag containing the guns out of the car and headed inside. Loco was standing in front of the two niggas with gloves on. Their faces were busted up, eyes swollen, and they were leakin' like shit.

"Damn, you couldn't wait for us to get here, my nigga?" I shook my head at Loco.

"Fuck no, these lil' bastards kept muggin' me like they was 'bout that life." he replied. I walked over to the two niggas and started my line of questioning.

"So, y'all work for Maurice, right?" They both nodded.

"Now, we won't hurt you depending on how you answer my questions. Now, I know niggas in movies make being tortured look easy, and they be willing to die before they talk. That's shits not true; being tortured is painful as hell. I mean, I like to inflict pain if that's what you want, but it works best for the both of us if you just talk." I told them.

"Now, did Maurice have some of y'all go to D.C. and hit some trap houses?" I asked.

"Yeah, he had two of his hittas go do it, that's how he got his start." the one with the closed eye replied.

"Do them niggas be around?" I asked.

He nodded yes. "They come to the house every day to check on the money." he continued.

"So, I take it that you run the trap." I pointed at the nigga that wasn't talkin'. He nodded yeah.

"Who is yo supplier?" I asked.

"I don't know; he deals with some nigga in D.C., and him and his girlfriend Alexia or some other nigga name Anfernee drop it here." he replied.

Loco and I looked at each other. Alexia was the person who the car that followed Venus was registered to, and Anfernee was one of the niggas we killed that tried to kidnap her.

"So now Frank using Maurice to take over a new city, huh?" I thought, not realizing I was speaking out loud.

"Frank?" the guy questioned. "Maurice is building his own empire; he said he's tired of living under his father and not being respected. I'm his right-hand." he stated proudly.

"Nigga, the way y'all in here singing, you ain't got the heart to be right-hand, just like Maurice." I looked this lil' scary bastard dead in the eye.

"When is yo next meeting?" I inquired.

"He just supplied us, so we won't meet until we need to reup." he replied.

"Aye, I need the three of y'all to search this place and take everything." I told Smoke, L, and D-Boy.

While they were going through the house getting all the money and merch, me and Loco was beating the shit outta these niggas just for being lil' bitches.

Normally, I would kill the niggas after beating their asses, but I wanted these niggas to live to tell the story; this shit was personal, and I wanted that to be clear. Knowing that I was taking over their shit, it wouldn't be too long before them niggas came at me, and I wanted them to. I wanted them playing my game on my field. I would have home court advantage, and it wouldn't be shit for me to take them out.

We took the lil' bitches with us until we was ready for out next move, their trap. Loco knew what time they had their daily meet, so we waited until then to make our move. We sat outside and watched the niggas gather in the house. I asked the so-called right-hand if that was everybody, and he nodded yes.

"Nigga, if you lying to me, I'll cut yo fuckin' heart out. I don't want any surprises." I warned him.

Not that I cared about surprises, 'cause I had enough muthafuckas to make sure we saw whatever was coming. I had the nigga D-Boy to stay with the niggas while the rest of us ran up in the house. Gutta kicked the door in.

"DON'T MAKE A MUTHAFUCKIN' MOVE!" he shouted, point his AK around at everybody. Loco, L, and Smoke followed him with their shit drawn.

"Aight, I want all y'all guns in the middle of the floor right now." Gutta said as I came in the door with my nine at my side. Loco started checkin' them niggas, making sure they had no more weapons.

"Anybody even look funny, I will dead yo ass!" L shouted, mean muggin' them niggas. After making sure them niggas had nothing else, I grabbed a seat and sat in the middle of the floor.

"I want all the money and product that's in this house, including what you have in your pockets. I will have you searched and if I find anything on you, yo life ends today." I spoke with authority as theses niggas started emptying their pockets. After collecting everything in the house, it was time for me to lay down the law.

"From now on, y'all niggas work for me; if I find out that y'all got any type of merch from anybody else, I will come back and murk each and every last one of y'all, you feel me? Y'all niggas don't eat unless I feed you; think I'm playing, let me give you a small example of what I'm capable of." I signaled Gutta and he signaled D-Boy. He came in with the so-called right-hand and the other lil' bitch, and threw them on the floor.

"See, this is nothing compared to what I really do; now, do y'all niggas understand? This my shit now." They all nodded their heads looking at their leader with a horrid look.

I kneeled down next to the so-called right-hand.

"Call yo boss and tell him everything is gone from all y'all spots, and tell him the nigga who did it said a dog will hold his head down when he do something bad, but a snake would look you dead in the eye; he will know what that mean."

I looked around at all of them. "Don't make me come back."

I walked out.

Maurice

I can't believe how fuckin' sexy Alexia makes pregnancy look with the way her little baby bump looks in that long sundress dress. She definitely got me ready to give her this dick. I watched her juicy lips move as I tried focusing on what the fuck she was saying.

"So baby, are we going to Ocean City this weekend still?" she asked.

I moved closer to her and started kissing her neck. She was tryna push me away, still talking, but all I wanted was her ass bouncing up and down my pole. The more she talked, the more I wanted to snatch her lil' ass up and stick my dick down her throat; my ass was so fuckin' gone off her. I slid my hand up her dress and rammed my fingers inside of her pussy.

"Maurice are you paying any attention to me?" she asked, sliding down on the bed and giving me full access to her wetness.

"What the fuck is the problem? You interrupting my mommy and me playtime?" I snapped.

Alexia shook her head. "You so fuckin' freaky." she giggled.

I leaned over top of her and kissed her, twirling my tongue around in her sweet tasting mouth. She let out a moan that vibrated in my mouth, causing my dick to get hard. The buzzing of my phone interrupted my mood. I was thinking I should ignore it, but something told me to answer it.

"Maurice, dude! They hit one of the spots man, and they made off with the stash and now trying to take over your spots," Havoc frantically spoke into the phone. "Man, they snatched OUR SHIT! Niggas can't serve their blocks? Nigga out here been acting stupid." he added

I couldn't believe what the fuck I was hearing.

"FUCK!" I shouted. My blood was boiling, and a nigga was ready to air theses stupid muthafuckas out. "All I wanna know is HOW IN TH FUCK DID THEY GET OUR FUCKING PRODUCT!" I yelled into the phone.

"Some niggas came up in here; they fucked me up bad, and they took everything, and—" he started, but I cut him off.

"Unless you telling me how you 'bout to stop this fucking takeover, fuck whatever the hell you think you 'bout to spit at me," I said. "GET THE FUCK OUT AND GO HANDLE THIS SHIT! You bitches need to have y'all bitch asses on the streets airing these muthafuckas out! They taking food out y'all mouth and y'all think shit's sweet? Is this what the fuck we do? Do you think I bust my fuckin' ass to allow another muthafucka to tell me when to bow down? FUCK NAW!" I was pissed the fuck off.

"But Maurice, it's some niggas you know 'cause the boss told me to tell you that a dog will hang his head when he do something bad, but a snake will look you in the eyes; he said you would know what that mean." This nigga sounded like he was about to cry and shit.

I had to take a pause to get my shit together. I knew exactly who it was that hit my shit. I didn't know how the fuck he found out, but I was gon' have to put an end to his ass.

"FUCK!" I yelled into the phone; as hard as I worked to get to this point, and this nigga came and took my shit.

"Havoc, I got this; just chill the fuck out until it gets handled." I spoke a little calmer.

"What's wrong, baby?" Alexia sat up on her knees on the bed, rubbing my shoulder.

"Adonis went to Detroit and took all my shit." I grimaced.

"What the fuck you mean Adonis took yo shit? How the fuck do he even know about Detroit?" she questioned as she hopped off of the bed. "Oh Shit! Do he know about me?" she asked in a panic.

"I MEAN, HE TOOK EVERY FUCKIN' THING!" I yelled, then took a deep breath to calm myself; I didn't mean to holler at her. "I don't know how he found out, and I as far as I know. he thinks your name is Raquel, but I don't know if he found out your real name or not, shit I have no clue how he found out about anything." I answered.

"I don't believe this shit; why in the hell is this nigga still living and breathing? He fuck up everything for us. We couldn't even kidnap and get rid of his bitch without him intervening." She fumed. "FUCK HIM!" she screamed. "I hate him so much; he treated me like shit, but treats this bitch like she's the fuckin' queen of England or somebody."

I understood Alexia was just as pissed off as I was, but her rant started to sound a little more like jealousy.

"Alexia, are you jealous of that bitch? Why in the hell do you want Venus gone so bad?" I wondered.

"Because Maurice, if it wasn't for her, we would have been in a better position and we wouldn't be in this situation right now; yo plans wouldn't be taking so long. I had Adonis right where I wanted him, just like we planned. If this bitch didn't keep throwing herself on him then he wouldn't have found out about Detroit and we could have been set up for the takeover." she shook her head "Had I known everything was gon' get fucked up, I would have kept handling him by myself." she raged.

"Alexia, I'm the one who provided you with the money to help you keep up with yo fucking charade; you think I planned on falling in love with you? No, that just happened. Now you having my baby and I'm so happy, and I promise you gon' have everything I told you we would; I just need to figure shit out. I can't skim from my father, so right now I don't have SHIT!"

"Adonis got to pay." she said in a low tone.

"Yeah, I wasn't tryna make this personal, but he just did. Since he in Detroit fuckin' up my shit,

I'ma fuck up his life; he ain't here to protect his bitch now." I smirked.

"She gon' die today."

Venus

"Kay Kay, why don't you just take the damn test? Stop stressing and you don't even know if you're pregnant or not; you might not be for all you know." I popped the trunk and took one of the grocery bags out.

Kay Kay reached into the trunk and pulled out a bag.

"What if I am pregnant, Venus? I don't want a child right now, and we both know how Loco feels about having a child; he don't want one, not in his lifestyle anyway," she said.

"Yeah, well he felt the same way about a relationship but look at y'all know," I reminded her. "I mean, he loves you; I'm sure things are gonna work out." I bumped her with my hip, tryna cheer her up a little. We were walking up the driveway, and she stopped short.

"How do you deal with this, Venus? You have a child and one on the way; on top of that, you yourself almost got kidnapped. I can't deal with shit like that with a child, having a constant threat on our lives." She sounded really worried.

"Kaylee, me and my girls are fine. Harmony is always happy as hell, and this little one in my stomach is doing great; just take the damn test before you go all in a panic," I chuckled. "Look, they will be home tonight; just sit Loco down and talk to him."

"I guess I will; this is sickening. But what about my career, Venus? How am I gonna be able to continue my career? It's just getting started." She looked at me with her lips poked out.

"I'm doing it. I had a child and again, I have one on the way and I'm just getting started in the same career; remember, we doing it together." I assured.

We continued to walk up the driveway. I stopped on the steps and turned toward her and said,

"Kaylee, you're gonna be a great mom; look how you are with Harmony, she adores you."

"Yeah, but Harmony is my goddaughter, not my daughter. I'm not responsible for raising her." she replied.

"Stop worrying so much; you don't even know if you're pregnant yet." I laughed.

We walked into the house and placed the bags on the kitchen counter, then we went back out to the car to get some more bags.

"So, did you send Adonis pictures of the house you found?" she asked, changing the subject.

I was glad she did because I didn't want her to keep worrying about a baby when she didn't even know if she was pregnant or not. I hoped she was; I would love for our kids to grow up and be best friends like us.

"No, I decided to wait and show him when he gets home tonight." I replied.

I opened the trunk again and got another bag out. I got a slight pain in my back and grimaced, grabbing my back.

"Should you be carrying that?" Kay Kay asked with a look of concern, making me laugh.

"Girl, I'm pregnant, not handicapped; besides, it's just growing pains."

"Venus, gimme those bags girl, what's wrong with you? You shouldn't be carrying these bags." Mrs. Thompson stressed, taking the bags out of my hands before I could get in the door good.

"They're not that heavy, ma." I shook my head; she was always fussing over me.

"Any more in the car?" she asked.

"Yeah, it's three more in my trunk but I can get them." I answered.

"Chile, sit yo ass down; always running around here cooking and cleaning and shit. You need to chill the hell out sometimes." she said.

"I know, Mrs. Thompson. I tell her the same thing, but she won't listen; she thinks she superwoman." Kay Kay agreed with Mrs. Thompson.

"Well, her ass gon' listen today. I'ma go get them bags and she gon' sit here and relax. I'll be right back." She started to go out of the kitchen.

"Mrs. Thompson, I'll help you," Kay Kay offered, getting up from the table.

"Chile, I don't need no help; how you think I keep my girlish figure? It sho ain't from sitting on my ass all day." She placed her hands on her hips and did a quick twirl.

Mrs. Thompson really did look good for her age; her honey color complexion complemented her small, sleepy-looking chestnut eyes very well, and her tiny athletic frame was toned and perfectly proportioned with her B-cup breasts, but her ass was a little too plump for her small structure.

"Ma, stop showing off." I laughed "Thinking you cute with yo vain self," I continued.

"Girl, if you don't think you cute, who else will?" She turned on her heels and headed out the door to get the rest of the groceries.

"Girl, Mrs. Thompson a mess." Kay Kay laughed as she started putting away the groceries.

"So, are you getting Harmony tonight or is she staying with your mom?" she asked, leaning in the refrigerator.

Before I could answer, gunshots rang out.

POW! POW! POW! POW!

"OH SHIT!" me and Kay Kay shouted in unison, then we ran out of the door.

I ran down the driveway and Mrs. Thompson was slumped over in my trunk, she was shot in the back, and blood was dripping down my trunk and onto the bags of groceries.

I shrieked and rushed over to her; she was still breathing. I yelled for Kay Kay to call 911.

"Come on ma, be ok, please!" I cried.

Two neighbors came over to try to assist me, but there was nothing they could do but wait for the ambulance like me.

"OH MY GOD, OH MY GOD, OH MY GOD!" I kept repeating as I sat in the driveway with my hands over my head, rocking back and forth.

By the time the ambulance arrived, Mrs. Thompson was unconscious, even though she was still breathing and had a pulse. Once they slid her onto the gurney, the paramedics hooked the oxygen onto her, then lifted her into the back. As soon as they pulled off, I broke down and started crying hysterically.

"Venus, come on, we got to go." Kay Kay said as she and the neighbor helped me up and into her car.

She put my seatbelt on the sped out of the driveway. I felt numb, but I knew I had to call Adonis. I took my phone out of my pocket and scrolled to his number. I closed my eyes as the phone started ringing.

"I am leaving the airport on my way home now." he answered.

As soon as I heard his voice, I burst into tears. "No, go to Southern Maryland Hospital, it's your mother; she's been shot!" I wailed into the phone.

"What the fuck you mean my mother been shot? Where was she? How is she? What the fuck?" His voice was wobbly as he continued firing off questions before I could get a word in.

Kay Kay

Shit like this is the reason why I don't want a child while Loco is still in this lifestyle; it's scary as hell. Venus sitting here looked disembodied, staring at the wall with her knees pulled to her chest, rocking back and forth. I can't stop trembling; I can't deal with this shit; it's too much.

"Doctor, please tell me something. I can't take this not knowing; please tell me anything." Venus begged the doctor for information with tear-filled eyes.

"I'm sorry, I can only give information to immediate family; that's the policy." he stated.

Adonis and Loco came running down the hall just as the doctor was walking away from Venus. I had never been so happy to see them in my life. I ran and jumped into Loco's arms.

"Doctor, I'm Adonis Thompson, Hattie Thompson's son; how is she? Is she ok? Where she at?" Adonis' voice trembled as he inquired about his mother's condition.

"She was shot four times in the back, and although none of her major organs or anything major was damaged, we had to place her in a medically-induced coma, and we can't be certain of anything until she comes out of it." the doctor informed.

"Can I see her?" he asked. His voice was brittle and almost childlike.

The doctor led them down the hall to her room. I looked up at Loco and gave him a kiss.

"You ready to go home?" he asked.

"Yeah, I'll call and check on them later." I replied.

The ride home was silent; I was still tryna figure in my head if I should tell Loco that I might be pregnant, or if I should just take the damn test like Venus said. I wasn't sure how Loco was gonna respond to me telling him that I might be pregnant, so I decided to just take the test first.

I was in the bathroom pacing the floor over and over, waiting for the results of the pregnancy test. I was nervous as hell. A few minutes went by and the timer pinged. With trembling hands, I reached for the test on the countertop.

"Shit!" I said, looking at the test in my hands. I couldn't be pregnant.

I shook my head knowing I should've been more careful, but when Loco got going, I wasn't thinking about no got damn condoms. I heard the bedroom door close, then I heard Loco's footsteps getting closer to the bathroom; my heart start pounding as sweat beads formed. I felt hot and started fanning myself with my hand. Loco jiggled the doorknob.

"Kay Kay, why the fuck you got the door locked?" he shouted from the other side.

"I'll be out in a second!" I called out with a tremulous voice. I was scared as hell, but I need to tell him now. I took a couple of deep breaths as he jiggled the knob again.

"Kay Kay, open this fuckin' door now! What's wrong with you?" his voice boomed through the door. I wiped my sweaty palms on my jeans.

"Ok Kaylee, you can do this." I coached myself.

I walked over to the door and unlocked it. Loco came barging into the bathroom. I quickly hid the test behind my back.

"What the hell wrong with you?" he asked, noticing the tears rolling down my face.

I didn't respond. His eye darted around the bathroom until they landed on the empty pregnancy test box on the counter. I rushed over to the counter and tried to block him from seeing it.

"What's that?" he asked.

I didn't respond, so he moved me out of the way. He looked at the empty box, then back at me with a puzzled look. I held up the positive pregnancy test.

"I'm pregnant." I announced. Fear grew all over his face.

"What the fuck you mean you pregnant?" he asked, looking at me with a distorted face.

"Loco, I mean I'm pregnant." I reiterated in a low voice.

Loco

"Kay Kay, we talked about this, you know how I feel about having a child. How could you let this happen?" She looked at me like she was offended.

"How could I let this happen?" she repeated.

"You know what I mean, Kaylee; why wasn't you being careful?" I asked.

"Why wasn't I being careful?" she repeated what I said again. "Wow Loco, what a reaction, just blame me." She stormed past me.

"How the fuck did you think I was gon' react? You know I don't want a child now." I followed her into the bedroom.

"You right, I know you don't want a child, and I didn't expect you to be all happy go lucky, but I didn't expect to be the blame when I never saw you slide a condom on your dick." she spat.

"You never asked me to either, did you? You could have been on birth control; how the hell was I supposed to know?"

"Nigga, did you ever ask me? Did you ever think to at least pull out? Hell no, all you thought about was getting that nut." Kay Kay was fuming, but I was too.

"Man, fuck what you talkin' 'bout? This is what you want; you wanted a relationship, I gave you that, but I guess that wasn't enough for you." I exasperated.

"Fuck you, what the fuck you think, I trapped you? Nigga, I don't need to trap yo ass." she said with a twisted face as she mushed my head with her finger.

"You want the family, the man, the child, the whole nine yards, and you know I'm not tryna give you all that right now; that's all I'm saying." I sat on the side of the bed and grabbed a blunt out of the drawer. I started gutting the blunt so I could roll me a jay. I really needed it right now.

"Loco, let's get this straight. I never pressured you to give me the whole nine yards; I'm not ready for that myself. F.Y.I., I don't want this baby either." she told me before storming out of the room and down the steps. I thought about what she said for a few minutes, then I followed her down the steps.

"What the fuck you mean you don't want this baby either?" I asked, confused.

"You heard what the fuck I said, I don't want the baby either." she reiterated.

"So what you saying, Kay Kay?" I didn't know if she was saying that she didn't want to have my baby or not, but for some reason it felt like she was.

"You don't want a child because of your lifestyle, and I don't either." That shit really hurt. I felt like she just reached in my body and snatched my heart out.

The truth was, I would love to have a baby with her, but I wasn't in the right mindset to be a father. I was still tryna get the relationship thing down pack, but hearing that she didn't want a child was really fuckin' with my brain.

"So what, I'm not good enough for you to have a baby by me?" I asked.

"I'm saying I don't want a child, that's all." she replied, taking a breath and exhaling like she was frustrated.

"You don't think I would be a good father?" my voice was low as I spoke. I was really hurt, and I never felt this way before.

"First, you blow up at me and blame me for getting pregnant; now, you wanna stand there looking like you just lost your best friend, but yet you don't want a child. You so fuckin' confusing right now, but none of this shit matters anyway because neither one of us want this baby, so I won't have it—simple as that." I looked at her like she had lost her mind; honestly, I thought she did.

"What you mean you not having the baby?" She said I was confusing, but her jumping from mood to mood was confusing the hell outta me.

"I mean I am getting an abortion, that's what the fuck I mean." She rolled her neck, crossing her arms over her chest.

I couldn't believe those words rolled off her tongue like it meant nothing to have an abortion. Yes, I killed for a living, but I could never harm, let alone kill a child. Why in the hell would she kill my seed?

"Kay Kay, you not killing my baby." I said in a low voice. I had my eyes closed, trying to fight the anger that was growing inside.

"Like hell I ain't. I am calling and making an appointment first thing in the morning."

She started to go upstairs acting nonchalant, and my anger surfaced. I grabbed her arm and snatched her off the steps, and backed her against the wall by her throat.

"Don't play this game, Kay Kay; you will lose. You will not kill my child or I promise that God would be the only thing saving you from being put in the dirt." I threatened.

"You like throwing that threat around, don't you? Well Loco, if you gon' kill me, do it and get it over with 'cause you not gon' keep threatening my fuckin' life." Her eyes held no fear as she stared deep into mine. I loved Kay Kay to death, and it's no way I would ever hurt her. I released her from my grip.

"Get out." she said in a low voice.

"Kay Kay, don't kill my baby." I pleaded.

"GET...THE...FUCK...OUTTA... MY.... FUCKIN'...HOUSE!" she yelled each word, making sure that I understood.

"Kaylee—" I started, but she cut me off

"GO NOW, LOCO." With tears in both of our eyes, I walked toward the door.

"Kay Kay, please don't kill my baby."

She slammed the door in my face.

Adonis

"Ma, I'm so sorry this happened to you. I can't lose you too," I cried as I placed my head on her bed.

Seeing my mother hooked up to them machines and knowing that they were the only thing saving her life right now had me fucked up in the head. This was all my fault; if I hadn't gone after Frank then my mother wouldn't be lying in the hospital fighting for her life right now.

"Ma, I promise I will never put you in this situation again. I love you so much." I held her hand in mine as I sobbed. I wiped my tears away, but every time I looked at my mother laying in that bed, I cried all over again.

I laid my head in her lap and started thinking about her singing the song she used to play all the time when we were young, Otis Redding's "Sittin on the Dock Bay." She would put that song on and pull me up.

"Come on, boy; dance with your mama," she would say, doing her two-step while snapping her fingers.

I heard the song playing in my head and I started singing.

Sittin' in the mornin' sun / I'll be sittin' when the evenin' comes / Watchin' the ships roll in / Then I watch 'em roll away again, yeah

I got up and started doing her two-step and snapping my fingers

"Come on ma, dance with yo boy," I chuckled, then continued singing.

I'm sittin on the dock of the bay/ Watchin the tide roll away, ooo/ I'm just sittin on the dock of the bay/ wasting time.

I danced for a few minutes, then collapsed in the chair. I took my mother's hand in mine again.

"Ma, please. I lost Lavelle, I can't lose you. I swear I'm done...ma. Please don't leave me." I heard the door open and close. I looked up and Frank was standing there staring at me.

Fuck! I thought to myself.

I looked at Frank, then back to my mother "Do whatever you need to do, Frank."

Frank walked over to the chair and sat down. "I just wanna talk." His voice was calm.

I was in no mood to talk, but I wasn't gonna let shit pop off in my mother's room either, and I wasn't about to disrespect her; besides, I would see him soon.

"You know you had me fucked up for a while, hittin' my traps the way you did." he stated.

I snickered in disbelief. He had the nerve to come in here and tell me I fucked him up when he was responsible for my brother's death and my mother fighting for her life.

"How the fuck you gon' come at me on some *I had you fucked up* shit? You fucked up my life when you killed my brother." I raged.

"I didn't kill Lavelle." I took a deep, calming breath. "I loved Lavelle like a son; he was loyal to me. I didn't kill him, I had no reason to." The tone of his voice held a hint of sadness, and for some reason, I believed him.

"Frank, Lavelle told me about your last meeting; he said you thought he was stealing your money, and you said you had to clean house, even if it hurts. If you didn't kill him, who did?" I inquired, tryna get the truth out of him.

"Adonis, you just like your brother, worst even. I been watching the way you move since you started in this game. I see your brother taught you well and you learned quickly. Your brother tried to do the same with my son, but Maurice ain't built for this life. I don't know why Lavelle couldn't see that. That meeting was me coming to the realization that my own son was stealing from me, and as much as I love Maurice, I can't save him from the inevitable. I knew the first time he came to me informing me that Lavelle was stealing from me that he was planning something. That meeting with your brother was my way of figuring out what Maurice was doing."

"I know what he was doing. I felt that Maurice was dirty for a while and I had him investigated; he was the one responsible for hittin' the traps and yo club. I recently found out that he was setting up camp in Detroit, so I went there and shut him down, and I found out that he never had a deal with Rojas. I spoke to him myself. The one thing I can't figure out is who Alexia is, and what she has to do with all of this."

"Alexia used to be a dancer at my club by the name of Fantasy; you should know her real well, Adonis."

"How should I know her? I wasn't in your club like that." I was confused.

"She was your girl; now she's his girl, and she's carrying my grandchild." he informed me.

"Raquel?" I asked. He nodded his head yes. I couldn't believe that bitch was playing me the whole time.

"Frank, I'ma be honest with you; your son is coming for you, just like he killed my brother, tried to kidnap my pregnant girl, and now I know he is responsible for my mother being in here. Why are you here?" I asked.

"The only reason I haven't retaliated on you and killed you was because I knew what you was thinking, and you were hurting just like me. I was waiting for an opportunity to sit down with you and talk to you man to man without us killing each other. I thought that we can figure out a plan to take care of Maurice."

"Frank, Maurice is your son, but the only way I intend on takin' care of him is ending his life; now, if you have a problem with that then we can end this conversation right now."

"Do whatever you need to do; if he really coming after me, I have to treat him like I would treat any other nigga—get him before he gets me."

"Well, I have a plan." I told him.

After telling Frank my plan, we figured out how to put my plan into action. Sitting down with Frank was definitely not what I expected, but I was glad I did. Now I knew the truth, and now I could dead Maurice without worrying about Frank coming for my family.

Frank stood up and shook my hand.

"Thanks for the information, I see you have the same type of loyalty as your brother. He was a good man, and I miss him a lot." He walked away, but before leaving out of the door, he turned to me and said, "You know after this is over, you gon' pay me for destroying my shit."

"I got you," I chuckled.

"I'm praying for your mom. I hope she pulls through."

He turned and walked out of the door.

Maurice

It's about fuckin' time, my pops finally giving me the respect that I deserve. He called me today and asked if I could go with him to meet a new connect. He never invited me to a meeting. I guess after all this time he can finally see my value to his empire, and maybe he knows now that I can run a tight ship just like him. Lavelle was his golden child, but he's dead now. Pops has no choice, but I'm cool with that. Thanks to Adonis I needed a new supplier anyway. Adonis was becoming a thorn in my side and I couldn't wait to body him. Once that's done, pop's empire is all mine. Instead of meeting my pop at the meeting point, he offered to give me a ride. That was out of his character as well.

On the way, the ride was silent. Pops ain't much of a talker anyway unless he's pissed the fuck off, then the nigga won't shut the fuck up. I looked out of the window and saw a billboard of a man holding a baby. I thought about Alexia, I can't wait to hold my baby in 6 months. I'm gon' be the father I never had.

"What you over there smiling about boy?" pops asked.

"Just thinking about being a father," I replied. "Maybe I can get some advice from you when the baby comes."

"Yeah that's cool," He replied.

We pulled up to my pops warehouse and parked in the garage. Something was off and didn't feel right.

"Yo pops, who we meeting?" I questioned.

"This nigga I heard a lot about, he offering a better deal than Rojas, and since shit was funny with Rojas, I'm looking for a new supplier." He stated.

We walked into the empty building, pops looked at his watch to check the time. I shook my head. I can't believe this nigga think I would fall for this set up shit. This the same shit I did to Lavelle.

He the boss, but he has to take a page out of my book, a nigga with no heart. Fuck this I'm tired of waiting for my turn.

"So you must really think I'm stupid." I said.

"What the fuck are you talking about Maurice?" Pops turn around and came face to face with my 9mm.The look on his face was priceless.

"Maurice what you doing?" He looked at me confused and somewhat annoyed.

"You would never take me on a meeting with you, you don't respect me, you don't think I have the heart." I laughed. "Well pops the jokes on you."

"Maurice what are you talking about?" he asked with a puzzled expression on his face.

"I was the one behind all the hits, the money coming short, and your precious Lavelle's death. See, I been planning this for a long time. I wanted to kill you and take your empire. Only thing standing in my way was Lavelle. He was too fuckin' loyal and as smart as he was, he didn't see me coming. You just couldn't believe Lavelle would steal from you. The truth is Rojas didn't want to deal with me, he wanted Lavelle. Everybody wanted Lavelle. Even you, you wished he was yo own son, not me."

"Maurice that's not true." He tried to sound sincere but I could see through his bullshit.

That pissed me off, he couldn't even admit that he hates me.

"IT IS TRUE!" I pinched the bridge of my nose as the anger that I held for so long came to surface.

"You never cared for me, you said I didn't have the heart for this business." I laughed. "I have more heart than you thought, see you in hell Frank."

"PUT YOUR GUN DOWN MUTHAFUCKA" I heard Adonis voice echo throughout the warehouse, I could hear his gun cocking.

Hatred burned in my eyes knowing where my father stood.

"You chose that nigga over me, your own flesh and blood. You evil bastard."

POW!

The sound of my bullet going through his skull was satisfying. His blood splattered all over my face.

Adonis

Maurice put a bullet right between Frank's eyes, he smiled as Frank's body hit the ground, then he turned towards me with his gun on me.

"Maurice put the gun down, it's over." I said in a calm tone. He laughed.

"Adonis if you shoot me, you won't know what happened to your brother, so I suggest you put the gun down." He smirked.

I knew Loco was creeping up behind the nigga, so I made him think he had the upper hand, I put my gun on the ground.

"What happened to my brother?" I asked.

"Simple, I killed him. The night at the condemned building, I called Lavelle and told him that I found the nigga that was robbing the traps, and I had him tied up in the build. That part was true, but I lied about him being the robbing the traps, see Anfernee was in need of some fast money, he owed the wrong people. I paid his debt in return, I kicked his ass and made him sit in the chair like he was the traitor. It worked like a charm, but once Lavelle started fuckin' him up more than he already was, he couldn't handle it. I gave him the signal to tell Lavelle that it was me he was working for and as soon as he turned around I put three bullets in his chest, you should have seen him flopping around like a fish out of water, oh wait you did, he died in your arms right?" he burst out laughing.

I was standing there with my fist balled, nose, flared, I was seeing red.

"Why did you kill my brother?" I asked.

"Because he was in my way, and you always looking at me like you didn't trust me."

"I didn't." I cut him off. "I use to see you looking at my brother with a smug look or looking at him like you hated him, I knew you were jealous, just like I knew you were dirty." I mugged him.

"Yeah I knew you were gon' be up in my business, so I distracted you with Alexia, oh damn my bad Raquel, I paid her to keep you away, I never intended on killing you, I'm doing this for Alexia, she wants you and you bitch dead, I tried to make that happen for her. I had no clue that was you moms leaning in the car, she fine ass shit. Maybe after I take care you and Venus, I'll pay her a little visit in the hospital." He laughed.

I let him talk long enough, now he got to die. I blinked my eyes twice and Loco hit the nigga arm sending his gun crashing to the ground. He kicked it over to me.

"Now let's have fun." I said in a sinister voice.

Loco punch the nigga so hard his tooth fell out. we took turns beating his ass, then I took out a knife, and started stabbing his ass. Not nowhere that would kill I just felt like hearing the nigga scream bloody murda. I took the machete and sliced off his tattoo, like I was slicing through butter. His as passed out, Loco woke him back up.

"You can't sleep through this nigga." I smirked.

The torture went on for about another half an hour, then I had Loco sit the nigga and his broken up body, up.

"Rojas sends his regards." I said then used the machete to cut his head off.

I went in the back room and hosed off, then changed clothes, Loco did the same, being that we were covered in blood, then I called the cleaning crew. When they got there, I instructed them to personally deliver his head in a box to Rojas, and the skin of his tattoo in a box and address it to Raquel. I gave them the addresses then me and Loco left.

"I had so much fun fuckin' up that nigga" Loco said when we got in the car.

"I did too, but now it's time for me to go home and have fun with Venus." Loco got a weird look on his face.

"I miss Kay Kay." He admitted.

"Nigga, y'all gon' be fine, give her a few days then go talk to her, and stop threating to kill her." I shook my head.

I dropped that nigga off at his car and took my ass home. As soon as I got in the house, I hopped in the shower and changed into some basketball shorts and a t-shirt. Venus was sitting in the bed looking like she was deep in thought. I flopped down on the bed beside her.

"What's on yo mind" I asked as I rubbed and kissed her ass.

You know what I'm thinking about?" she asked.

"What." I answered.

"I'm thinking about when we first met and you stopped Mr. Li from calling the police on me you was so genuine and kind hearted. Remember our first date, you took me bowling because I never been before." She took my hand in hers the caressed the side of my face turning me to face her. Looking deeply in my eyes she continued "Remember how I couldn't contain my excitement when we were at the counter waiting for the guy to get our shoes."

"Yeah you kept peeking over the counter with a big goofy ass grin on your face." I chuckled at the memory.

"Yeah and you wrapped your arms around me to show me how to hold the ball and the correct way to roll it." she laughed.

"Yeah when you finally got a strike you jumped on me and made us both fall." She laughed.

She had me remembering how much I loved her, after all these years, she still makes me feel like that teenage boy. I grabbed her by her shirt and pulled her in for a kiss but she stopped me.

"No not like that, I want you to become that 16-year-old boy take me back to the night we lost our virginity to each other. You remember how you felt. tryna act like you was cool but you were just as nervous as I was."

"Yeah but that was years ago, we did a lot of freaky shit since that night. I could never go back."

She put her hair in a ponytail and slid up on the bed. I climbed on top of her and kissed her. I slid my hand down her body then started taking off her shirt. She grabbed my hands stopping me. "Wait." She sat up on the bed "Adonis I'm a virgin." She said just like she did the night we took each other's virginity.

I kissed her softly. her tongue fluttered against mine, while my hands were deep in the softness of her hair, and it was like time carried back to when we were teenagers I slowly removed her clothes, then mine. I climbed back on the bed on top of her. I looked into her amber eyes. she quickly covered her face. I smirked at how cute she looked. It was like time instantly transformed us back to we were teenagers. Mimicking everything, we did that night, I used my knee to part her legs. I even started feeling myself getting nervous when her rapid breathing turned into deep heavy pants as if she was petrified. I moved her hands from her face and took the hair bow outta her hair. She shook her head so that her soft curls would fall just like they did that night. I wanted to see her when I entered her. I could feel her chest rising and falling quickly underneath me.

"You ready?" I whispered. She nervously nodded yes. She let out a loud gasp when I entered her grabbing and my arms squeezing tightly.

"Ouch." She screamed digging her nails deep in my skin. I stopped thinking that I hurt her.

She laid there stiff as a board clutching on to me for life. her eyes were closed tightly, her mouth still wide open. I saw a tear roll down the side of her face. I wiped it away and kissed her.

As exciting as it was to role play the first time we had sex, I was tired of pretending like I didn't tear her ass up in the bedroom. I was ready to go in.

"Umm Umm Umm." She moaned loudly as I turned her on her side, put one leg up, gripped her hips, and went balls deep in her pussy speeding up my pace.

I could feel her body shaking uncontrollable as she let out a scream of passion and squirted all on me. I continued my stroke until all the built up tension that was in my body release in her along with my built up seamen. I collapsed on top of her and kissed.

"Marry me." I whispered in her ear.

"Adonis stop playing." She chuckled.

I reached over and got the ring out of the nightstand drawer.

"I brought this the day up told me you were pregnant before all that shit happened. My intentions were to propose to you that night. Venus I want to be with you for the rest of my life so I'm asking you, will you be my wife."

"Yes." She said in a low brittle voice as tears rolled down her face.

3 months later

Venus

"OH MY GOD!" I shouted as the contractions got stronger.

It was too late for me to get an epidural, and my labor was kicking my ass.

"Baby, go wet that towel for her and rub her head," Mrs. Thompson told Adonis.

"AAAAAAAAHHHHH!" I cried out.

I felt like I was ready to push this baby out. Mrs. Thompson grabbed her cane and came over and sat in the chair beside me.

"Just hold my hand, squeeze it when you feel pain," she spoke softly.

Adonis came back with a bucket of cold water and a towel; he placed the towel in the water and started dabbing my forehead. The coolness of the towel felt good on my forehead, but it was irritating the hell outta me; I slapped his hand away.

"Stop being mean," he chuckled.

Another contraction hit and I was squeezing the shit outta both of their hands.

"Breathe through, baby," Adonis coached as he started breathing with me.

When I relaxed, he started dabbing my head again. I closed my eyes and tried to ignore the discomfort. A few minutes later, the doctor came in and checked me; it was time.

"You ready?" he asked, and I nodded yes.

"Ok, when I tell you to push, I want you to give me a nice big push, ok?" he instructed, and I nodded yes again

"Ok, you ready? Push."

I pushed as hard as I could for as long as I could; that shit hurt like hell. Adonis had one leg and his mother had the other to help me push the baby out.

"Ok, Venus, you ready? Push."

I gave him a good push as Adonis and his mother held my legs back. A few more pushes later, five-pound 10-ounce Serene Jordyn Thompson was born. She was beautiful.

A few hours later, Adonis said that he was going to take his mother home and come back. I told the nurse to take the baby to the nursery so that I could go to sleep; I was exhausted.

****

"Hi, I'm here to see my baby."

The nurse was bouncing around the nursery scanning all the babies' hospital ID bands.

"Sure, I'll be with you in a moment, the shift just changed," she beamed.

"No problem, take your time." I really wanted her to hurry; I just wanted to feel my baby in my arms.

"Ok umm," she paused.

"Venus." I flashed her a smile. "That beautiful baby girl Thompson is mine."

"Yes, she is beautiful; let me just check your ID band." I held out my arm and she scanned the band, then my baby's band.

"Here she is," she chuckled as she placed her in my arms.

"Hi, mommy's beautiful baby," I smiled as I stroked her soft little cheek with my finger.

"Can I take her to my room?" I asked.

"Sure you can," she beamed.

I thanked her, then left out.

Adonis

"Hi, I came to see my baby," I told the nurse that was on duty. I hadn't met this nurse before, so I introduced myself. "I'm sorry for being rude. I'm Adonis Thompson, and Serene Thompson is my daughter."

She walked over to me and shook my hand. "Nice to meet you, I'm Tekeila, the night nurse, and mom already took the baby to her room," she informed me.

"Thank you Tekeila." I rushed to the elevator, eager to hold my precious daughter in my arms.

I was standing on the elevator wishing that it would hurry up. It stopped and the doors opened. I rushed out of the elevator and down the hall. When I got to Venus' room, she was laying in the bed looking half asleep.

"Where's Serene?" I asked, confused.

"She's in the nursery," she replied.

"I just left the nursery, and they said you brought the baby up here," I told her.

She sat up in bed with a frightened look on her face.

"Adonis, where's my baby?" she asked. I shrugged my shoulders

"The nurse said you have her."

Venus pushed the call button.

"WE NEED A NURSE!" I yelled down the hallway.

The nurse came rushing in the room

"Is everything ok?" she asked.

"Where's my baby? Did she go for any tests?" I asked.

"No, she was in the nursery a while ago; did you go there?" she asked, confused.

"I went there and the nurse said Venus came and got her, and she's not here; are you telling me that my baby is missing? Please tell me that's not what you're telling me!" Fear and anger were rising in my body at the same time.

"Adonis."

"What are you telling me, nurse?" I was tryna remain calm.

"Adonis."

"One minute, Venus," I blew her off.

"Nurse, don't make me get ugly in this fuckin' hospital—where in the fuck is my baby?" I raged.

"ADONIS!" Venus shouted.

"WHAT!"

"My ID band is missing."

TO BE CONTINUED...

Interested in becoming a part of

the Treasured Publications family?

Submit manuscripts to

Info@Treasuredpub.com

Like us on Facebook:

Treasured Publications

Be sure to text **Treasured** to **22828**

To subscribe to our Mailing List.

Never miss a release or contest

again!

CPSIA information can be obtained
at www.ICGtesting.com
Printed in the USA
LVOW13s2316151216
517437LV00014B/361/P